NOMAD'S FALL

BURNING BASTARDS MC
BOOK 2

BY RYDER DANE

This Work is fiction. All organizations, events, and characters named or referenced in this work are products of the author's imagination or used fictitiously.

ISBN-10# 1-945012-11-0

ISBN-13# 978-1-945012-11-2

Artwork by Jess Buffett Graphic Designs

Published by Vinvatar Publishing
Website: Vinvatar.com

TABLE OF CONTENTS

CHAPTER ONE

One day soon he planned to take some time off. He needed a vacation. Hell, he didn't really need to get away, he just needed something different. Being an Enforcer for The Burning Bastards MC was as exciting as it got within the club. Until the Bastards allowed the Chiefs to patch over, he and Demon had been soldiers in the club. They'd graduated to Nomads, or as some called them Enforcers, for a few years now, they normally traveled together on club business. Lately they'd drifted, the close friendship was not like it used to be. Now instead of both men going on a run, it was one man, and it bugged the hell out of him. He loved the job when there was work to be done. Right now, the only work he needed to finish was to find Dorsey, and sooner or later he would be found. The rat bastard was sanctioned as John Doe now.

Knight had just gotten back from yet another wild goose chase. He was hunting Dorsey, and every small lead had to be checked out. By the time he'd gotten to Conaway, Arkansas, the fucker was gone. The place was crawling with military personnel, and just being around the uniformed men and women while they gassed up their vehicles at the same place he'd filled up the Triumph made him feel guilty for leaving the service after his second tour. It took a few hundred miles on the road for him to blow the guilt off. He'd done what was necessary at the time for his mental health. He was becoming a twisted sonofabitch at the time, so much so the sight of death stopped bothering him and he started taking chances that should have killed him. The turning point for him was when two newer soldiers decided if he could do the dangerous shit and live through it, they should be able to as well, after all they were twenty-two and bulletproof right? Either they hadn't listened to their training, or they thought youth and arrogance would save them. One was a freckle faced redhead and the other was Nordic blonde. He was the one to find their bodies, at least what was left of them. He'd also killed eight men that day to make sure they never killed another American soldier. The only way for him to recover the bodies was to go through the enemy, and although it'd taken all day, luck had been riding his shoulder. The downside of that luck was he kept shooting the men he'd already killed. He ran out of bullets and used their own guns to continue riddling their bodies full of lead long after they'd bled their last drops onto the desert sand.

He'd become even more hardened after that day, nothing stopped him from killing the enemy, if they could breathe, they could cause harm, and he was all about keeping the bastards from causing harm.

*****

He tossed the dart, hitting the bullseye square on, and took the cash Heckle handed him. "You're one lucky motherfucker, always hitting the pussy, even with darts eh?" The dartboard was made more interesting by the fact that someone had taken a picture of Sylvia's naked ass bent over to show her cunt lips and asshole. They'd taken the metal cage from the original dartboard and placed it over the picture, with the high score bullseye being in the middle of the pussy shot.

Heckle was one of the coldest men Knight knew. He was also the type to gamble the dimes from a dead man's eyes, even if he had to dig up a corpse to get them. He once bet the tranny he'd brought to the club late that night would seduce Demon into letting him suck his cock. That hadn't gone over well. Heckle almost won that bet, until the guy saw the size of Demon's junk and balked. He'd lost his sexy she male voice and yelled, "Fuck no," when Demon grabbed his head and shoved it toward his overly impressive prick. Demon almost lost his shit when he figured out he'd been romanced by a guy. He was homophobic to a fault, and Heckle was lucky to have escaped with his teeth still in his head.

The only time he didn't bitch about seeing another man's erect cock, was when he was sharing a snatch. He even admitted to liking the feeling of the friction of another cock massaging his between the membrane of a woman's asshole and cunt. Slapping balls hadn't been mentioned at the time, but he seemed to have no problems with that either. Knight was one of the few men Demon would share a woman with, and while he was sure there was more to the story, it was Demon's business and his life. They might be best friends, but some lines didn't get crossed, like asking your best friend if there was some kind of history.

The door opened behind him and from the look on Pinky's face, you'd think they were being robbed. Her mouth opened to scream, and his hand went to his waistband before he turned slowly toward the doorway. Demon was standing in the doorway with blood dripping in his eye, and a woman's bleeding body was hanging in his arms.

Knight put his .40 away and went to help. "What the hell happened?" He didn't look at the woman, he was concerned because his buddy was swaying on his feet. He noticed Demon was bleeding from more than his head. The fucker was losing blood faster than the head wound would warrant, if the pool forming under his boot was any indication.

He took the woman into his arms and yelled for Tiny and Tarzan to get Demon down to the table. "Someone call an ambulance, he's been shot, and it looks like he's lost too much blood for us to deal with here." The burden in his arms was moaning and trying to say something, but from the way she was gasping for breath, and the visible injuries, he'd bet her lungs were injured too. "Tell them there's a female injured too, erratic breathing, sounds like she's gurgling, so I think it's her lungs." He could see she was starting to go into shock, but there wasn't much he could do for her without medical equipment, and even then, if he tried to drain or re-inflate her lungs, and that wasn't the problem, he was opening the group to a hell of a lawsuit.

He laid her on another table and told Heckle to watch her, "Just keep her from thrashing around or moving too much, she's in bad shape." He needed to find out what happened. Demon was awake and coherent. He wanted a bottle of whiskey, but Knight refused. "No, buddy, the alcohol will just make the blood flow faster. Tell me what happened, and who did this."

*****

The ambulance showed up faster than they expected, but the Prospects at the gate said Demon had told them to call the ambulance when he'd stumbled up to the checkpoint.

Big Dog wasn't in the area. He and Future were two hard days ride away dealing with some legal matters, and Demon had been tapped as the go-to brother when Butch's old lady went into labor early. That in itself had been a bad deal. She hemorrhaged and nothing the doctors did or tried worked. She passed away, leaving Butch with a set of twin babies to deal with and a dead wife to bury.

There were seven men left that he could easily tap until Big Dog got back. A quick call to Big D appointed Poppa and Tiny as backup for Georgie who was the club's Sergeant at Arms. Knight and Needles were given instructions to increase the hunt for Dorsey. "Find that cocksucker, if you can bring him into us that's a plus, if not, drop that fucker where he stands. We'll be back on Tuesday. They've lifted the cement and blacktop from the parking lot and found two more bodies. Future is having a hard time of it. Especially since she took a pregnancy test and it was positive. She's emotional, and it's pissing her off," said Big Dog.

"Hey, man, congratulations. That's wonderful. Give that gorgeous ass of hers a kiss for me. Happy for the two of you," Knight told Big D on the phone before they hung up.

8

During Church later that day, Knight brought up Big D's directive. "Find him, no matter what rock he's hiding under or river he's crossed. We want this bastard and we want him dead. Show's hunting for him now, so I gave him a ring, and he'll be back tomorrow. He was happy to hear that Dorsey's back in the area. Brother wants him bad, so you might not want to be standing between them when Show finally gets his chance."

Georgie told them, "That sewer rat was waiting for one of us to drive by. He shot Demon, and kept his finger on the trigger. That girl saw his scooter go off the road, stopped to help him, and Dorsey ran her down in a black truck while she was trying to pull Demon off the pavement. The cops found the truck a mile or two from where Demon was shot. Both the bike and the woman's car are DOA with bullet holes. Oh yeah, her name is Barbara Collier, some of you might have seen her before. She's twenty-seven, brown hair, blue eyes, works at the tire place in town. No word on her condition."

Georgie was a good man, he was to the point and didn't let much faze him, but he cautioned his brothers to be careful. "If that sucker is using a sniper's rifle, he'll probably be a few hundred yards out. Remember, he's a coward and won't give a shit who he shoots while he's at it."

While the rest of the men scattered to talk amongst themselves, Knight talked to Needles. "Dorsey must be camped out either in a house close by, or roughing it in the woods. Maybe in one of the lake cabins people use, like old man Bean's place." His money was on a cabin, not in town, there were too many people in the town that would sell him out the minute he showed his face. His bike would also be a dead giveaway. "The bastard is too fuckin' stupid for description, why stick close when he knows he's been tagged?"

They walked into the bar and could see the sluts from town had come by to slum with the "Dirty Bikers" that would give them what their pussyfied boyfriends wouldn't. They were all dressed up in skin baring clothes and make-up, trying to act sexy to attract a "bad boy" so they could brag about the experience later. One time a bridal party of women showed up and the bride showed her skills to the entire room. Knight smiled at the memory of fucking that wide ass of hers, while Demon fucked her cunt and she licked on Juicy's hairless snatch. That slut had been determined to get all the memories she could before locking down with the well to do "twerp" as she called him. As far as he knew, she hadn't been back since.

A pretty Amazon Queen with sleek muscles and long limbs slinked up to him at the bar in her fuck-me heels, wearing the shortest dress he'd seen in a while. Her hair and make-up suggested she knew she looked fabulous. He grinned and looked at the beauty's neck. "Sorry, darlin', I don't ride a trike" he nodded his head toward Heckle, who was watching the various women hopefully. "You see that big old boy over there? He's gotta dick that will split you wide open if that's what you're looking for." Queenie grinned, looked toward Heckle, and winked at Knight, before sauntering toward her new target. He wasn't outraged when he was approached by a man, he'd never admit it out loud, but he considered it kind of flattering. It wasn't his thing, but hey, he wasn't going to throw bricks at them either. Some of the most beautiful women he'd ever seen were in fact men.

He heard a high-pitched scream, and looked over to the small dance platforms the club's bitches used to entertain the men. There was a woman between the two poles holding on for dear life as Donnie and Pressley double fucked her ass and cunt. A scene he and Demon had played out many times over the years.

Fuck, he missed the closeness of their old friendship. He knew they needed to talk, and maybe with Demon being laid up, shot, he'd be able to mend his fuckup. He had to skirt around the oldsters on his way out the door.

Poppa, the second oldest greybeard of the club, was sucking on Cherry's tits, and her bony ass was grinding down over his prick, while Joker sat next to them waiting his turn. Seeing the old men still having hard dicks at their ages gave him hope for his own future sex life.

*****

Gladys was happy to see someone drive in. Visitors had been few and far between since Ralph died three months ago. People they'd known for years came to his funeral. Most of them that came from out of town had stayed here at the campground. When they left, they seemed to think she didn't mind cleaning the cabins and sucking up the cost of their weeklong vacation. The only good thing about being left on her own was that she had something to keep her busy. She often wondered what they would do if she sent them invoices for their stay.

Future had been a Godsend in her time of need. She had worked by her side to get the property ready for the summer season. Her mother, Muffy, had taken over the camp's website, and had really done an outstanding job with it. One of the best things to have come from the unusual friendship was that she'd learned to ride a motorcycle. After riding on the "bitch seat", she decided she had to buy a bike of her own. She had a sweet 383 Sportster. Not the biggest bike she could have gotten, but she loved it. Future told her she'd want a bigger motor eventually, but she was still getting used to the feeling of freedom as she drove down the open road. She had her license, but no plans for a long road trip yet, so Daisy would be enough for the little she'd be riding this summer. Much to Big D's chagrin, Future often brought her back to the clubhouse for lunch or parties during the daylight hours, and Daisy, with the bright yellow tank and fenders, disgusted him. Future's old man was a stick in the mud. If it wasn't black and decorated with flames and skulls, he hated it. That gave her the idea to use some stencils she'd found in the craft store. She bought paint from the local body shop, well she hadn't bought it actually, the guy, Mick, one of the Bastards, gave it to her. She'd shown him the stencils and told him what she planned to do. Once he'd stopped laughing, he handed her two small containers of paint and told her how to use them.

Daisy now sported ten skulls, red bows on top of each of them. She'd added the chandelier earrings and various necklaces to each skull as well. She could barely wait until her friend got back and she could show off the new, tougher looking Daisy.

Now she watched the two rough looking men dismount their bikes and heard their boots climbing the steps to the office. Gladys went to see what they needed. She was waiting at the desk when they opened the door. It wasn't until she saw one of the men was that rascal Knight that she lifted her hand from under the pile of paperwork. Now he was a man that could make her give up all pretense of her recent widowhood. He was well over six feet tall and had shaggy brown hair, wide shoulders, and an ass that was a privilege to watch walk away from a woman. When she looked at his companion, oh lordy.

He was tall and slender, with pierced ears and nose. He was young and if she hadn't know he was on the side of the good guys, she wouldn't be pulling her hand away from the 1911 under the papers on her desk. His tattoos and piercings gave him a menacing look and from the twinkle in his eyes, he knew the effect his looks had on people.

Knight started speaking, and she turned her attention his way.

"Hey, beautiful, how's it goin'?" Typical Knight, he was such a flirt, some woman was going to have her hands full keeping his leash tight.

"What brings you out here to the lake today, handsome? Are you ready for a vacation of fishing and sunbathing? We're taking reservations from next week into September. Now that I remember what your face looks like, maybe I ought to hire a few of you Bastards to sit down by the lake without your shirts on, take a few pictures, and put them in an ad for the place. I'll even let you keep your cuts on. Let's face it, a girl loves a man in leather with his tats showing. We're sure to get a whole summer booked with single women ready to take a walk on the wild side." From the looks of horror on their faces, she had to laugh. "Come on, guys, just think, you could come up here, get all the tail you could want, and I would have a full campground all summer long. Sounds like a win-win for all of us." Needles was watching her and she could see he was trying to decide if she was messing with them or if she was serious. She opened her mouth to elaborate, but Knight cut in on her finale.

"The answer is no, and stop trying to confuse Needles here. He's tender, and you might hurt his feelings making fun of us like that." He shook his head at her antics. Gladys was a different kind of woman that seemed to listen to her own music most of the time. She was a pretty woman around forty with bleached platinum hair that spiked all over her head, and she gave back any verbal shit as good as she got. Georgie got his leathers all sweaty every time he saw her. They had a love-hate thing going, and Knight privately thought they deserved each other. Ralph had been an odd duck, but she had married him and buried him, and now three months later, she was showing her own personality.

"Well I figure you're here to bust me for the shooting of your brother yesterday. In my defense, I was making the rounds and found someone trying to shoot Cujo. I heard shots, and drove the golf cart down to find out who was disturbing the peace. I couldn't get close enough to see him, and when I shot him, it was an accident. I was aiming next to him, and he jerked to the side when he went after Cujo. I was just trying to scare him off. When he turned and fell, I saw his patch. I think the bullet hit him in the ass." She blushed, thinking about her embarrassment at shooting someone she hadn't intended to shoot. She threw up her hands, "I don't know what the punishment for shooting one of your boys is, but he was trespassing and trying to kill my goose. He left faster than I could get to him, so he can't be hurt all that bad."

The news got their attention. She was expecting Knight to do something, she didn't expect the deep grin and laughter. "What?"

"The asshole you shot wouldn't have been six foot and a buck ninety-five would he? Driving a dark green hog, wearing a bandana to cover his grey hair? If it's him, that's what we came to see you about. He's not someone you want to fuck with, Gladys, he will hurt you and laugh while he hides behind a kid. The man is a coward, and a killer. If he comes back, hide and give me a call." He scribbled his number on one of her business cards, and handed it to her.

"I didn't see him good enough to tell if his hair was grey or his weight. I saw a man raising a gun toward a helpless animal, and probably should have yelled at him first, but I got trigger happy and shot him on accident instead. I know I hit him because he dropped to his knee and was limping badly as he ran away. There was blood on the sand where he'd been standing and, wait a minute." She ran back into the house and came back with her arms full of a blanket wrapped around the man's personal belongings he'd left behind when he took off. Needles reached over the desk and pulled the bundle over to his side. He was grinning and looking at her with something close to respect.

"I'm not joking, Gladys. The number under mine is a brother named Show. If you can't reach me, call him. He wears nothing but black and looks a little scary, but if you can handle us, he'll be easy. I'll call him and give him a heads up."

The men left and she enjoyed the scenery as they walked away. The information about her trespasser worried her. Hopefully the bikers would find the man before her guests started to show up in eight days. If he was still in the area, he'd be back looking for his things. She felt the tingle in her spine.

Old habits came back to her from memory, and she knew what she needed to do. Fingers crossed, she still had the ability to get the job done. She and Ralph had been two of a mercenary group working to help the downtrodden in the world. They'd left the group of assassins that specialized in covert activities around the globe. Since they'd retired, they still kept their hands in the protection of certain high profile people. The campgrounds were perfect for the safety of those individuals. Two of the cabins were equipped with steel reinforced walls and drop down window shields for protection. For the past five years, there'd been no problems to worry about.

When they weren't needed by the protection group that called themselves Necessary Evils, ordinary vacationers enjoyed the modern cabins for a higher price than their more rustic counterparts.

CHAPTER TWO

Jolly Baker was driving along praying to the fuel fume gods to let her get to the next town before she ran out of gas. She needed to find employment and a place to live for a few months until it was time for her to move on again.

She planned to sell the oil burner as soon as she had a job and transportation, like a city bus system or a Dial-a-Ride kind of setup. No need to buy insurance and add another bill to have to pay, not to mention the lack of a paper trail would make it harder to follow her. The car ran out of gas and fumes five minutes later, and she had no idea where she was.

There was a wooden sign advertising "Big Lake Campgrounds" fifty feet in front of her, but that was about it. Not even a road mile marker could be seen. *If I didn't have to use back roads and goat paths I'd at least know where I was*. She got out of the old Olds and looked around, but that didn't help, there was nothing to see. After standing with her car for half an hour with no vehicles passing by, she grabbed her purse and locked the doors before heading in the direction of the campground's sign.

It was close to dark by the time she walked up to the manager's office. The closed sign on the door was just one more disappointment in a long line today. Yesterday she'd barely escaped from being snagged by sneaking out the back door of the truck stop where she'd been working. She'd slipped into her studio apartment, aka attic room in a slumlord's

1900s Victorian, via the fire escape. The dark blue SUV parked half a block away was about as inconspicuous as a black eye. How she'd been found was anyone's guess. She grabbed her duffel, stuffed her pitiful belongings into the cheap bag, and pulled up the carpet in the corner of the room to get her small cache of money.

The car was in a fake name, with fake plates and for a derelict, it had at least gotten her a few hundred miles away, so she couldn't complain too much, but it drank gas at what seemed to be ten miles per gallon.

She had changed her hair color two months ago, and now she'd have to do it again. At this rate, she wouldn't need to worry about her hair, it would be so brittle, it would all break off and she'd be bald. She thought her appearance had changed drastically enough to keep her under the radar, but there was no guarantee about that either. She'd been a kick ass college student with dreams of owning her own business and seeing her name on the side of her own building. While she attended her normal college courses, she'd gotten licensed as a Massage Therapist to supplement her income. It was originally her idea to get out of the Lady, and find work in a Chiropractor, or Doctor's office. She couldn't use her skills for that without showing her license, and that had been left at her mother's home. Even then, if she used her real name so an employer could check her out, that would leave her trail wide open for her pursuers. That was over two years ago. Now she was a woman running scared from some very bad people with no place isolated enough to keep her safe.

Sitting on the wooden steps and crying her eyes out wasn't going to improve her situation any, but that's exactly what she did. No wimpy crying jag for her, it was an all-out blubbering release of emotions and tension. She hadn't cried since the night she discovered her boss was a killer. She would have slipped away scot-free if it wasn't for the damn security cameras. She'd been in the office waiting to tell her boss at the Lovely Ladies strip club, that she needed to change her working hours due to her class schedule for the year.

A man begging for his life wasn't something she expected to hear coming from the backroom. Nor was the sound of a single gunshot, and a few minutes later, the sounds of something heavy being pulled across the floor. She'd snuck out of the office and ran to get her purse, explained to the girls in the dressing room that she suddenly didn't feel well and needed to go home and lie down for a while. The next day Porter came to her door.

She lied to him, denying she spent any time in the office last night at all. "I did go into the office looking for you last night, Porter, but you weren't there, so I left. I wanted to tell you I'm moving to Denver to start a business, and give you my two weeks' notice. I feel it's only fair since I've been with the place for three years."

His two 'friends' hadn't believed her, but she allowed tears to leak from the corner of her eyes, and told him how much she was going to miss the club and the people in it. She told him she was so grateful for being employed for so many years, and so on. Porter bought her performance, his friends stood back and relaxed until he left the shabby room. The last man out of the door turned to her and grabbed her shoulder, pulling her close to him. "I can smell a lie from fifty feet away. I'm going to be watching you. Porter may have a soft spot for you, but I don't have soft spots. Remember that."

She managed to walk back into the place that night and the following twelve nights, each time wondering if she'd be allowed to walk out on her own, or if she'd be rolled up in a carpet. She couldn't let them know she was spooked, but it was hard to keep a smile when James watched her so closely. His constant staring made her clumsy and scared out of her mind. The girls made her a cake and gave her gifts as going away presents on her last night at the strip club. Porter hugged her close and whispered in her ear as she was leaving the building. "Get in your car, drive, keep your mouth shut, and change your name. Act normal, but get the hell out of town, take only what you need, and don't look back." She smiled a sickly grin and took the small package he held out to her.

The girls came outside to see her off, James standing behind them, still watching as she drove away. She spent ten precious minutes in her apartment gathering only what she could carry, and left the bedroom light on when she walked out. Her car was a flashy little VW and she loved it, but it had to go if Porter's warning was a real threat. She had no reason not to believe him. She left it in the airport parking lot and hoped it wouldn't be discovered for a few weeks. The four thousand in her savings account was pulled out as soon as the branch opened for business that morning.

She pulled her hair into a ponytail and slapped a ball cap on her head for the bus ride that would drop her off in Memphis. From there, she picked a random town in Ohio to ride to next. She bought a one way ticket to Denver and found a homeless woman on the street that obviously had a drug problem. After bribing her with a joint laced with crack, she watched as the woman set out on her new adventure to the land of "all the weed I can smoke and not be arrested." She had two hundred in cash and was as high as a hit would take her. The baseball cap and ponytail was clearly visible for the security cameras to pick up. The hoodie sweater had been a favorite, but it served a better purpose now.

From there she rented a hotel room, walked to the corner drug store and bought scissors and auburn hair coloring. Thankfully the desk clerk understood her tearful explanation that she was hiding out from her abusive boyfriend, and would rather not have her license number on the register. She was using the name Fern Jordon then. She found a small apartment in Chicago, where people only walked around at night if they were armed, and willing to risk their life.

That place had lasted the longest. For four months, she came and went as she pleased, until the local drug dealer decided she might be a threat. He visited her one night, and was quite serious when he told her to pack her shit and leave.

She learned a few things about men and sex that night. She decided she was a freak for not knowing until then. Him and his associate, she'd never forget. Not that they'd worried, but she went to the County Health Department to get tested for STDs in Idaho. She took a repeat testing panel when she made her way to Arizona. Just to be on the safe side.

Every time she saw a dark blue SUV with tinted windows she got spooked. She knew she needed to take a stand somewhere, but where could she go that those bastards wouldn't find her? More importantly, how were they finding her? Was the driver of the SUV even James, or an innocent family out for a drive? She'd stopped calling her mother months ago, worried they were tracing her calls. She was so paranoid that she carried a semi-automatic in her waistband and one in an ankle rig when it was possible. That skill had been accidently acquired, but once she tried to kill milk jugs filled with food coloring in water, she was hooked on shooting. She decided she was only slightly psychotic to go with that pesky case of paranoia, and she learned to hit what she was shooting at.

The door behind her rattled, and she jumped, wiping her face with one hand and reaching behind her with the other hand. A woman's face appeared in the window, and the door opened. "Come on inside, rain's coming and you're about to get drenched. I hate when that happens, even if it's the best time for a woman to cry like you were. The rain helps cleanse the misery away. At my age I can tell you it's the truth. I do it myself once in a while when things get overwhelming."

Jolly followed the woman who introduced herself as Gladys. "Have a seat, my dear, I just brewed a pot of French vanilla coffee and planned to sit on the screen porch to enjoy it. There's not much to do around here right now, at least not until next week. The campers will start trickling in by then. I'm sure you need a job, and from the looks and sounds of your heartache, I'd say you're running scared. The bathroom's through that door if you want to wash your face. I'll poor the coffee and meet you out on the porch."

She was thankful for the lady's discretion. Her bladder was about to burst, and she felt much better once she took care of that problem. She picked a washcloth from the stack in a little wicker basket next to the sink and washed her face, it was odd how she felt she could trust this woman. Stupid, but still the feeling was there. There was something so solid about her and Jolly wanted nothing more than to tell her everything that had happened to her in the past two years. She would have to watch herself, or she'd blurt out the entire story.

Gladys knew the girl would lie to her, *but the truth will come out*, it almost always did. Her friend, Future, wasn't the only one around these parts with a certain ability, people felt her inner calm, some called it empathy, and blurt out all manner of secrets. It was one of the skills that made her a valuable asset in her former profession.

"Thank you for opening the door, I ran out of gas a few feet from your sign up on the road and since the sign was the only thing I could see around, I followed it to here." She sipped the hot brew and felt it warming her from the inside out. "This is great, thank you."

Gladys sipped from her cup and set it down next to her. "So, let's get to the story you've decided to use, so you can break down and tell me the truth sooner than later. I'll start okay?" She smiled at the younger woman.

"You ran out of gas, just passing through the back of beyond, and thought it was a shortcut? You're running from an abusive boyfriend? How about you just needed to change your life, and decided this area would be a good place to find a life." She picked up her coffee mug and sat back, waiting to see what the girl would do.

"I can't tell you the truth, I can't tell anybody, if I do, then they might get hurt. You're a nice lady, but I can't do that to you."

Gladys shook her head. "Did it ever occur to you that if something happened to you, something bad like you're afraid of, no one will know who to look for? Your family will always wonder what caused your death. You look like a scared rabbit, and bad men like to corner their prey to torment it until it dies of fright, or sinks its teeth into their skin, knowing they will die, but refusing to give up hoping for a miracle. And before you start running again, let me tell you a few things about me. Things no one in this part of the country knows.

"I was an ordinary kid, grew up with an ordinary family in an ordinary neighborhood. When I graduated from high school, I went to college and did my damnedest not to be ordinary. I got my degree, and joined a team of extraordinary people. We were supposed to change the world. I saw murders, I saw child pornographers, and I saw so many inhumane things that no one should be forced to see. I cracked when my partner was shot in the back by a sniper and I ended up shooting the man to save Ralph's life. I killed a few more men and a woman before I realized I wasn't going to save the world, especially when it doesn't seem to want to be saved.

"Ralph and I were not in love, neither of us believed in that emotion. We married to pool our resources and buy this place together. There's not one soul in the world besides you and me that know that story." She took another swallow of coffee. "Now, it's your turn to talk, but if you plan on lying, don't bother. I only told you my backstory, in case something happens tonight, or in the near future. That way someone will know."

Jolly was so confused by the woman's confessions that she wondered if any of it was true. She watched as Gladys punched a button on her cell phone.

She called the local garage and after a dozen rings a grouchy Beadle answered. "There's a car on the county road just down from my place." She looked toward Jolly and asked what the make and model was. "She says it is an 87' Olds, just call here when you show up and we'll meet you. Bring a can of gas please. What do you mean to talk like that? Beadle, I hope you don't talk to your momma that way, 'cause if I was your momma, you would be eating soap right now."

"Thank you for calling, I don't have a cell phone anymore, and had no idea what I was going to do." She knew it was time she told someone about her problem. The woman was right, if James caught up with her, who would know what happened to her, or why. As long as she didn't give the name of the club or anything, she should be able to trust that none of the information would get out, right?

She was so tired of living like she had been. The release of her emotions earlier on the front steps seemed to have helped her come to terms and straightened out a few things for her. She could take a stand, or she could keep running.

Gladys sat watching her, and the words just seemed to spew out of her mouth. She heard herself explaining why she didn't go to the police in the first place. "Cops come in that place and get star treatment, everything from free drinks to free time in the back rooms with some of the girls." She shook her head, "I wouldn't have lived for ten hours if I'd gone to them." The other woman showed no judgment, she was actually nodding her head.

"I can't figure out how they keep finding me, or if I am just being paranoid, but I can't take the chance. James is a scary bastard with dead eyes."

"There's only one way they could be finding you. You must be carrying something with a transmitter, like a chip they use on dogs. What'd you bring with you from your old life? Think about it, right now we should get the golf cart and start up the road. I have lights on the buggy, but it's dark out, and Beadle isn't the sharpest knife in the drawer."

After an hour of sitting at the end of the drive to the campground, Beadle still didn't show up. By then Gladys was good and pissed. She punched some numbers in her phone. "You call that miserable little fucker at the garage, and tell him I said to go fuck himself. Leaving a woman on a deserted road, knowing she needs gas, and I called the little bastard over an hour ago." She listened to whoever was talking on the other end of the line for a minute and although she couldn't be certain, Jolly imagined smoke radiating off the woman's head.

"You know what, Mr. Big Bad Biker fuck, you can kiss my fat ass too. Don't bother dragging your delicate ass out into the nighttime air. Call your boy and cancel, I've already called Merles, they said they'd be here in twenty. Have a nice night, asshole." She punched the screen, and smiled at Jolly. "Let's go gas up the car and get it into the barn." She reached back and pulled up the tarp revealing a five gallon plastic jug filled with gas. "I use this for the lawnmowers and chainsaw."

They got the vehicle started, and Jolly followed the golf cart back to the barn. For some strange reason, relief washed over her when the door closed behind her junk car. She felt safer than she had in months. As they waited for Beadle, Gladys offered her a job at the campground for the summer, and after that, they'd see what direction she should take.

It was close to eleven at night by the time they'd determined Porter's parting gift was the giveaway to her whereabouts. Gladys used a small wrench that she usually used for her winter craft projects to remove the back from the gold and diamond watch. There was a small disk under the back case. The watch was a kinetic, and it didn't need a battery. "Here we go, this is your homing device. They must really want to keep tabs on you for some reason. Are you sure all you did was strip? You haven't forgotten a lover or something?"

"I think I would have remembered something like that. My last relationship was in college, when I was a sophomore. When he found out what I really did for a living, he freaked out. The only thing I've had since that, that even resembles sex was a close encounter with a drug dealer named Mr. Grim. Trust me when I say I would never imagine how fucked up some men are. He was in the mood to drive his warning for me to leave the neighborhood in a very effective way."

CHAPTER THREE

Knight knew Georgie must have had words with Gladys again. The man had Vicky on her knees, and his hands were holding her head steady ready for his prick to drive deep into her throat. He came with a roar and staggered back to his chair without bothering to zip up his jeans. At least his prick had retreated behind the denim so they weren't subjected to the sight of Mr. Squirmy. Vicky stood and gave him a dirty look. She wiped her mouth with the back of her hand and walked away.

"Well, brother, that makes what, four of the Bitches you've pissed off? You keep this shit up and the only pussy you might get is on the weekends when the sluts and round heeled party girls show up." Georgie gave him the shit stare, but it didn't faze him anymore. "I went up to Big Lake campground today. We have a sighting of Dorsey, and I hafta say that Gladys is a hell of a woman. She shot him in the ass when he was trying to kill off one of her pet geese. She didn't see any particulars, but she saw the Bastards patch when he turned and limped off." He laughed at the thunderous look on Georgie's face. "She shot him in the ass or the leg. I'm voting on his ass."

Georgie shut his eyes and lifted his face heavenward, probably asking for patience.

"She took his kit from the beach, handed it over to me and Needles. His phone, a bundle of gold chains, and a thousand in cash. We got his saddlebags and blanket too. I told her to be careful, he's gonna want his shit back. She told me she'd be fine, but I think we should set someone to watch over her for a few, just in case."

Georgie had it bad since he'd met the snappy little bitch. Even knowing she was married to Ralph hadn't phased his interest. She was short and a bit stocky, but she was sexy as hell, and he'd wanted her too long to chance close contact now that she was a free agent. Hell, she'd just buried Ralph a few months back. If he came onto her now, she'd always think of him as an even bigger asshole than she already did. He wanted to go to her and keep her safe, just in case Dorsey developed a worse case of stupidity. He wanted her safe as much as he wanted Dorsey dead.

After tonight's call from Gladys, he wasn't sure if he even stood a chance with her once she was ready to see another man anyway. "I just talked to her. She seemed the same bitchy woman she always is. I'm not sure what Beadle is thinking, but he pretty much blew her off when she called the garage for someone to do a gas run for a stranded woman on the road by her place. She says to tell him to fuck off, and she didn't want to listen to me telling her the boy was probably too busy to cater to her at the snap of her fingers. She called me a biker fuck. Gladys doesn't talk like that."

Knight signaled for two more beers and thanked Pinky for bringing them. One went to his inebriated, love struck friend, and he drank the other one. "Face it, man, women are hard to understand. A man can give her his money, a roof over her head and food for her belly. It's not enough, they aren't

31

happy until you lock down and hand her your prick and the hammer to smash your balls with." He clinked longnecks with Georgie, who kept nodding his head at the philosophical viewpoint.

"Look at Butch, that poor sucker is fucked, he doesn't see it that way, loves those cute little babies. I was there with him when his old lady died. That was one miserable man, he had the doc by the neck, and I had to pull him off. Lucky for all of us that pretty little Asian nurse gave him a shot while I held onto him. That calmed his ass right down." He took a long pull on the beer. "Butch is in bad shape, and says he's the one that wanted the kids so soon after they married. He's blaming himself for her dying."

The two of them talked about how men got tangled in a woman's web one way or the other. There was no escaping it, if a woman had her sights on a man, he was as good as screwed if she was half decent looking, and he liked her to begin with.

Georgie passed out sitting up, and Knight took the empty bottle from his fingers. He figured it wouldn't hurt to take a drive by the campground first thing in the morning, just in case there'd been any problems overnight.

He made his way to one of the backrooms, instead of going home or to the bunkhouse. He needed to run into town to check on Demon, and find out if there was anything they could do for the woman that'd been hurt trying to help him. Maybe he'd check in with Butch and see how the poor bastard was doing while he was in the area.

*****

Jolly came out of the room she was given to sleep in to find the bathroom. She saw a figure in black walking down the hall in front of her. She slipped back into the room and pulled the .9mm from its nylon holster.

Gladys heard the slide snap, *How did he get behind me in the hall?* and realized it must be her houseguest. "Jolly, it's me, don't shoot for crissakes, and don't turn on the lights." She slowly turned and saw the girl still held the pistol trained on her, and wanted to praise her for being smart. There wasn't time to have the heart to heart right now, not if she wanted to find Dorsey before he came back and found her. "I'm going out for a while, and I'll be back in a couple of hours. There's something I need to check on, and now is the best time for me to take care of it. Just stay inside with the doors locked, when I get back, we'll talk." She turned around and kept moving.

Jolly followed her and watched Gladys open the closet in the dining room and step inside. "You might as well come in here, you'll be curious when I leave and snoop anyway." The woman was right, she would have opened the door and looked inside once she'd left.

The right wall of the walk-in closet was open, and Gladys was bent over a computer keyboard clicking away for a few minutes. "What's going on here? Gladys? I do know how to shoot a gun, I own two of them. I've had to learn to be sneaky and hide in the shadows myself, so let me help you. Just tell me what we're hunting for and I promise I won't slow you down."

Two monitors with four picture frames showed up on the screens. Gladys was studying each square carefully. "I'm not worried that you'll slow me down, I worry about what you'd do if I have to kill this guy. He's dangerous and some friends of mine are looking for him in the area. He kills people and when he gets cornered, he's a damn coward. He was on the property yesterday and I shot him in the ass on accident. If I aim a gun at him again, and he makes me shoot him, it won't be an accident this time." She stood and turned around.

Jolly got the picture then. Gladys was dressed in black, her head was covered in a nylon hood that was snug against her neck and somehow blended into the black cargo pants and long sleeved figure hugging shirt. She was wearing black hiking boots and the wide belt on her hips sported a knife in its sheath, two small black leather pouches, and two guns in holsters. The slots for extra clips on the belt were filled, and a small LED flashlight hung from a loop. She looked like a Power Ranger, minus the cartoon aspect, and the color accents. "What are you, an assassin?"

Gladys shook her head, "Not any longer, I admit the suit's a bit tighter, but I managed to squeeze into it. Let's just hope I can still hunt as good as I used to. Now, you can watch the perimeter, on these monitors. If you see anyone moving, I want you to hit one of the keys one through eight. It will tell me where the activity is on the property so I can find him faster. I have my phone on vibrate, and silent, so don't bother trying to talk to me, I won't answer the phone. Got me?" She spent a few extra minutes showing Jolly how to pan the view and the zoom features. "I have three numbers written down next to the tower over here. If I'm not back by daylight, or haven't called you, call the first two numbers. If they find me dead, call the last number on the list. Whatever you do, don't call the last number until you see my dead body for yourself. Can you do this?"

"Of course I can do this, a trained bear could do this. I'll be here, but don't play the hero okay? You are the first potential friend I've met in two years, I need you alive." Jolly was still confused, but now she had a mission, and she would help this crazy woman. After she came back, they were going to talk all right? Everything she wanted to know would be cleared up. She wanted to beg Gladys to come back, or let her go along, she did neither of those things. Truth was, she'd probably throw up if she saw another dead body. Just like she had thrown up when she'd killed a man on the highway in Utah. He'd been a bad guy in preacher's clothing. She'd killed him with his own gun while he was trying to rape her in the backseat of her broken down car. It was another time when she had to move on fast, and was four hundred miles from putting another state between her and James, when the water pump blew. It was nighttime and he pulled his car in behind hers. He was all smiles and expressed such concern for her plight that she began to trust him to help her. She'd opened the back door of her car to get her duffel and he was on her. She ended up badly beaten and bruised, before she got her hand on the snub-nose .38. He told her, "It's not personal, all you whores need to be tenderized before a man can take a good bite outta your hide." His beefy hands had been around her throat, cutting off her air supply, when her flailing hands encountered his revolver. She'd torched both cars where they sat. That night she learned to swim. There was a small river between her and the cars on one side, and an open field on the other.

Now she sat watching the screens almost afraid to blink because she might miss something. She played with the zoom feature and the gadget finally hit pay dirt as far as she was concerned. A small campfire was barely visible in the section marked with a number seven in the picture. She quickly hit the number and continued to watch that panel more than the others. No matter how she zoomed the lens, she couldn't get anything better as far as the picture went. She watched the other screens to make certain there was nothing else to concentrate on. She was concentrating on the screens so hard the sound of breaking glass made her jump.

Shit. What happened? It couldn't be Gladys back yet. She'd only left an hour or so ago. She left the small space and shut the door to keep anyone from seeing the light from the monitors, and peeked around the closet door. Her gun was in her hand, ready to use and it was a good thing too. She could see a large male figure stumbling around the wet bar in the dining room. He was drinking from a bottle of something and pouring another on the beautiful wooden surface of the bar. He lit a cigarette and she heard him give a low laugh. "Fuckin' bastards." He belched and looked around the room, but he didn't bother to look at the closet door. He walked into the kitchen and she followed in the shadows. She crouched behind the low wall between the kitchen and living room. He dug through the fridge and pulled out half a chicken. From the little she could see from her hiding place, he was scarfing the thing down as if he was starving. He took one hand off the chicken and reached for the bottle he'd been drinking from. The grease on his fingers caused the bottle to slip through his fingers and drop onto the hardwood floor. "Fuck, that was some good shit."

He continued eating mouthfuls of chicken as he stumbled back to the wet bar. She had nowhere to go. If he bothered to look down, he'd see her. She held her breath, not daring to move an inch for fear it would draw his attention to her. He dropped the chicken carcass on the floor and started yelling, "Hey you motherfuckers, get down here and show me to my room. You thieving bastards took my bed, so I'll fuckin' take yours for the night." He upended his newest bottle and when he brought it down, his eyes must have seen her crouched there. His mistake was not seeing the gun in her hand. He reached for his side and she opened fire.

She'd seen the gun on his hip when he was standing in the light from the fridge. From what Gladys had said, this guy was a killer. She felt nothing while pulling the trigger. He hit his head when he tried to run to the door, and fell hitting the corner of the table. He'd crushed a chair on his way down, but she knew he was hit by her bullets. She knew he was still alive. She hadn't made a kill shot.

His judgment wouldn't be coming from her. She might regret it later, but tonight he got a pass on his spot in hell.

She turned on the light above her, all the while keeping her finger on the trigger. If he twitched, he was dead. He was out cold and bleeding a hell of a lot from his shoulder, hip, and thigh. The head wound continued to seep blood, but it'd stop eventually, the cut wasn't deep or very big. She took several extension cords from the dining room closet, and wrapped his legs from ankle to knee. She had to roll his heavy body to tie his hands behind his back, and lifted the gun and knife from his belt. She sat back on her calves and took a deep breath. Jolly really wanted to push him onto the front porch, but there was no way she could move him. The nasty smelling man had to weigh close to two hundred pounds. She went back to the closet and looked over the monitors for some sign of Gladys. When she didn't see any trace of the woman, she took a chance and typed in a text on the computer. "Come Home NOW," was all she could think to say. After all, anyone might read the message and she wasn't about to admit in writing that she'd shot a man and he was tied up on the dining room floor.

She was exhausted, but kept busy cleaning up the mess the pig had made. She hated to do it, but she used hot soapy water on the wooden wet bar and hardwood floors. They didn't look any worse for wear, but you never knew. At least they were no longer sticky and greasy. She pulled a cardboard cereal box from the cupboard and left the cereal in the plastic, but used a kitchen knife to cut a square to cover the broken window in the office door.

The sun came up and she was terrified Gladys had been murdered before this animal had broken into the house. She went into the closet again, fiddling with the controls, and still she couldn't see any movement except the leaves fluttering in the breeze. Even the campfire from last night had disappeared. She felt funny using the old-fashioned telephone to call the first number on the list, but she punched in the numbers and waited for the line to be answered.

CHAPTER FOUR

She allowed the phone to ring twelve times before hanging up and dialing the second number. It was answered in six rings, and she still had no idea what to say to whoever answered. "Yeah" was not exactly a greeting, but she wasn't going to lecture the man on the other end of the line. "Um, I was told to call this number if Gladys didn't come home by morning, she's not here, and I'm worried. I'm sorry if I woke you, but the sun is up and she isn't back, and someone needs to go find her please. I tried calling the other number, but no one answered, and I, could you just hurry if you can?"

"Who is this and what do you mean Gladys is gone? Gladys was at home last night, if this is some kind of bullshit, I can guarantee you won't like it when I find you." She hit the End Call on the phone. There wasn't much she could do without knowing which direction the woman headed. The monitor started showing text across the bottom of the screen. "Need help, call Ge, northw."

She grabbed the phone again. When the rude bastard answered, she told him, "Look, asshole, I don't give a damn who you are or what you say you will do to me. Gladys is in trouble, she just sent me a text to call someone with the name Ge or G something, I need to talk to him, if you're not him, find him, and tell him to get his ass over here now." She punched the End icon and wiped her face with both hands.

The lump on the floor began groaning and cussing. He'd caused enough trouble as far as she was concerned and she kicked him in the ribs. "One more sound out of you and I'll finish the job." She bent down and checked to make certain he was still secure, and decided to add another extension cord between his wrists and his feet, just in case he thought he would find a way out of his predicament.

"You're the reason Gladys is out there somewhere needing help, and if I have to shoot you dead and go find her myself, I promise to make it painful. I'll gut shoot you and angle the barrel up, so the hydro shock will have a fun time ripping up your intestines and you can taste your own shit. I'll even gag you so you can hear yourself scream." She finished her roping skills and was happy with the result. His legs were now bent at the knee and the cord stretched his arms back so he almost balanced on his belly. After giving him another good kick, she went to the kitchen and brewed a pot of coffee.

For the next half hour, she alternated between filling her coffee mug and checking for any more communication from Gladys. She had the Walther pointed and ready to shoot the filthy bastard, so she could go and find Gladys herself, when she heard the roar of motorcycles. She looked out of the dining room window, and almost dropped the gun in her hand. There had to be ten big machines, most of them black and chrome, being parked in front of the porch. She ran over and opened the front door.

"Are one of you G?" The big grey-haired man stepping onto the board looked up at her and nodded his head. "Gladys is somewhere in the northwest corner of the property and she needs help." She made shooing gestures with her hands. The men stared at her like she had two heads. "Okay, I'll tell you what, you stay here with him," she gestured behind herself, "and I'll go look for her, just point me in the right direction." She turned away to find her shoes.

Georgie and Knight, followed by Show, who was actually called Freakshow, walked inside after the crazy woman wearing boy shorts and an oversized t-shirt that had bloodstains all over the front. She had blood on her cheek and her forearms, and several long streaks on her thighs. They heard her before they saw her, and could hear a man yelling at her to, "Just fuckin' shoot me you cunt." She was yelling at someone to, "Shut the fuck up," and kicking the hell out of the man lying on his stomach, hogtied. The mystery of where the blood came from was cleared up by looking at her toes. They were glistening with fresh, bright red, when she drew her foot back for another shot.

Show approached her and tried to take the gun from her hand without hurting her. She backed away and held the weapon in front of her body. Knight distracted her by shoving Dorsey's hogtied ass onto his side and laughing out loud. "Well, well, would you look at what she has here, all tied up in a nice neat bow. Show, leave her at it, she's done us a big favor and I'll be damned if she didn't shoot him too." She didn't relax as he thought she would.

"I told you to watch him, I need to change clothes and find Gladys. All I need is for one of you to tell me which direction is northwest. She's been out there all night and needs help."

Georgie stepped right up to the barrel of the gun. "Lady, I don't know who you are, but my name is George. You told Knight on the phone that she told you to call me. I'm here, I'll go find her and take most of my guys with me. You can take a shower and maybe try to get some sleep, 'cause if you were in your right mind, you'd know better than to point a gun at me unless you plan to use it." His hand came up slowly, and he almost had her, but she backed away and ran into the closet. They heard the lock click, and everyone breathed a sigh of relief.

Georgie went out to the porch leaving Knight and Show to deal with Dorsey. The seven men with George started trekking north. He was in the lead for the first half of the walk. He knew when the younger men eventually got bored following his old ass, they spread out, first flanking him, and soon passing him. The brush and trees got denser the further into the forested land they searched. At noon, he told them all to start heading west, and to double back the way they'd come. She couldn't have gotten this far in the middle of the night. It was broad daylight and he was sweating his ass off trying to cover the terrain.

Beacon yelled for attention, and he headed toward the sound of his voice. Unfortunately for him, he chose to cut across a thick patch of wild roses and the fuckers had thousands of thorns. His legs got caught in those damn things and he had to pull himself loose with sheer muscle power. The only tree large enough for him to grab a hold of was covered in poison ivy, and he knew better than to willingly put his hands on the stuff.

Georgie was one of the last to come up on the sight of Gladys lying over a small outcropping of rocks. He came closer and saw her right arm was bent at an awkward angle, and one of her legs was wedged to the knee between two of the larger rocks. She had a large lump on her forehead, and her skin, what he could see of it under the black camo grease, was pale white. Her body was shivering, and she was unconscious. His heart was stuck in his throat as he touched her face. "Oh, doll face, what in the hell were you thinking?"

The rock had to be moved, and it was a good thing he had all this young muscle with him or he'd be digging the rock out by hand. They ended up having to take a couple of sturdy tree branches and wedging them between the rocks under her leg. When they got the rock to move, he pulled her leg up and out of the small crevice.

"Tarzan, you take Beacon, get the speedboat from the campground and bring it over this way. I'd call an ambulance, but they couldn't get to her here. We'll have to get her to a place they can reach her as fast as we can. We'll follow the shoreline with her and you can pick us up." The men began the trek back to the lodge, while Georgie sat her upright, holding her head on his shoulder for a few minutes to let the blood flow better, at least that was what he told himself.

He kept her propped against him while he unbuckled the belt at her waist. The thing had to weigh ten pounds with the guns in his estimation. He handed it off to Needles. His doll face had some explaining to do.

*****

Show tormented the man he'd been hunting for months. "You gotta think of the irony here. You're always calling women "dumb assed split tails" and whores. Hell, you'd hide behind your own mother if she hadn't seen what you were, and had the smarts to kill herself. That female that brought you down might be a goddamned nutcase, but she had the smarts to shoot your ass. I like her style."

Big Dog and Future should be home by the time he got Dorsey back to the cells. He had a Louisville Slugger waiting for Big D's old lady to use if she still felt the need. He remembered that it had been her fondest wish. She declared she'd be satisfied if she had a baseball bat and Dorsey in the same room. Show was all about giving the woman what she wanted. After all, she'd encouraged him to follow his dreams and had put her money where her mouth was for him.

Heckle drove up in the double cab dually and Knight waved him down to the dock. Tarzan had just left in the speedboat to pick up Georgie and the rest of the search party, so they could transport Gladys to the hospital in the truck.

Big Dog showed up with Tiny in the panel van and backed it up to the front door of the office cabin. The brothers walked into the door and Show watched Dorsey's eyes scrunch closed, as his head dropped to the hardwood floor. "'Ol boy's not looking too happy to see you, Big D."

45

The big man was already hauling Dorsey's ass to the door. He dragged him by the cords wrapped between his feet and wrists while Dorsey screamed in pain at the wounds being reopened when the muscles became strained. "Keep screaming like the chicken shit fucker you are. I got someone that wants to have a reunion with you, and she's waited long enough." He kicked the bastard in the side and laughed at the knowledge that he'd just broken ribs, enjoying the new screams of anguish.

Tiny came around and helped him lift the bastard into the back of the van. He slid a noose around Dorsey's neck, and secured the end of the rope over the rack designed to hang bike parts. Big D went back into the building.

Knight was propped on the back two legs of a dining room chair next to a closet door. His hands were folded over his stomach, but his expression belied his relaxed posture showing it for the lie it was. "What the fuck is going on? I get a call for a pickup and see the gift you boys had for Future. Good capture by the way. And you look like you're waiting for a rat at a hole in the wall."

The chair legs hit the floor, and Knight stood, "Thanks, brother, but it wasn't us." His thumb indicated the door. "Got a call, mouthy bitch told me to get Georgie here on the trail of Gladys who was somewhere in the damn woods. We get here and this crazy woman with crazy hair and wild eyes, stood there waving a gun around. She's covered in blood, and Dorsey was already on the floor as you saw him. Georgie's in the woods with seven others, and I guess they found Gladys in rough shape.

46

They're picking her up in the speed boat." He finished his cap of the events and held up his hands.

"The crazy bitch is in the closet, hiding from us. She looks like she's about to drop from exhaustion or fright, something's off with her. She won't answer when I try to talk to her, but I hear a whimper every once in a while." He beat his fist on the door and they could barely hear the noise Knight talked about. "Get your ass out here."

He'd been waiting her out all day. It was getting to the point he was ready to rip the door off, but she had a gun, and she looked scared out of her mind. He didn't want to get shot for no good reason. Sooner or later she'd have to take a piss, or be hungry enough to come out on her own. He didn't want to hurt the fragile looking woman, but she would learn not to point a gun at a man unless she planned to pull the trigger. Remembering that she'd done just that was no comfort.

Big D gave him a disgusted look. "Knowing you knuckleheads, you probably came in here scaring her worse than Dorsey did. I know how Georgie feels about Gladys. Hell everyone knows but the two of them. Did you tell her they found Gladys, and that she's alive?" Knight shook his head, and Show tossed his hands in the air before walking away from the door.

Big D decided to do the honors himself. Future would hand him his nuts if he didn't help the woman that brought Dorsey down. He knocked on the door, "I thought you might want to know they found Gladys, and she's hurt, but she's alive. They took the boat to pick her up, and if you want to see

47

her before they take her to the hospital, you might want to come out of there. I'm Big Dog, and I lead the Burning Bastards. Gladys is a friend, and since you're her friend, you'll be safe. You have my word, no one will harm you." He waited for a minute. "Look, just come out and talk to me, you can keep your gun, we owe you for bringing down Dorsey."

The lock clicked and Knight shot him a dirty look. The door cracked open, and the two men could see bloodshot green eyes looking out toward them. She slid out the half opened door, and stood with her back to the wall. The gun in her hand stayed steady and she tracked the room with her eyes. "Gladys is all right, you swear?" From the looks of the bedraggled female standing on what had to be borrowed energy, he'd bet she was unaware she was covered in dried blood, and appeared to be one of those Zombie looking things. She was too slender, and the haunted look in her eyes made him ashamed of his friends. It wasn't like Knight to act like this.

"Yes, she's hurt, but Georgie and the brothers found her. She'll be heading to the hospital as soon as they get her off the boat. You and Gladys are both safe now, I promise."

She stared at him for another minute, nodded her head, and walked into the hallway. They heard a door open and shut.

Knight found himself up against the wall with his friend glaring at him. "You dumb motherfuckers ever terrorize a woman like that again and I'll kick your fuckin' asses back to the goddamned rock you came from under. That woman's in shock and she's frightened. You just seen the same fucking thing I did."

"Women do this. They're evil fucking bitches until the threat is over, then they fall apart if they feel safe enough to do it. That one never got the chance thanks to you assholes. Men like us, we relieve stress with sex and beating the shit out of each other, or shooting something. Women scream and cry. Future told me it keeps them from killing men." He looked Knight up and down, "I don't give two cents for your ass when Future finds out how you treated that girl. My advice is you exercise that charm you use to get women to drop their drawers, and fix this before my woman sees you. After seeing that girl, I'll even hand her the knife." He turned away and left the building.

Knight wondered what the hell that was about. He'd never done anything to the woman but wait her out. Well, beating on the door every fifteen minutes and demanding she come out might be considered terrorizing her. Seeing her in the light of day without the haze of worry about Gladys, and seeing Dorsey lying on the floor trussed like a pig ready for the spit, he felt like, hell, he didn't know what he felt like. Whatever it was, he didn't like being the bad guy here.

CHAPTER FIVE

Gladys had told her about her friendly relationship with the local badasses. Knowing they were supposed to be the good guys didn't instill any trust in her. The big handsome man they called Knight was an evil bastard. Twice she'd had her hand on the doorknob and each time his fist pounded on the door ordering her to get her ass out of the damn closet. Between the threats she felt from the older guy when he'd barked at her, and the younger man's actions since she hid in the closet out of fear, her nerves were in shreds.

She'd hoped to stay here for a while. Especially now that she felt so much less fear from James and Porter. Gladys had smashed the tracking chip with a hefty ball peen hammer, and tossed it into the burn barrel. She'd be free from detection now, and was grateful. She needed money, and she desperately needed a friend. Jolly prayed that Gladys was going to be all right. It was crazy and made no sense. She felt such a connection to the older woman, but had never met her before yesterday. Maybe because they'd shared secrets that no one else knew.

It still wasn't much of an explanation, but she was going with it. If Gladys wasn't able to return home to supervise, Jolly would be forced to find a job nearby and somewhere to sleep until she found a cheap place to live.

The sight of the hollow-eyed creature in the mirror might have horrified her, if she actually gave a shit right now. She planned to take a nap and hopefully by the time she woke, there'd be some word about Gladys's condition. She scrubbed the dark brown crusted rivulets of blood from her face and arms. Her legs, geez, crawling on the floor in the mess had painted the stuff on her. Her hair was another story, one best left ignored. It was too long to spike now, and the color was turning more muddy brown than the dark glossy brown with red highlights she'd put in a month ago.

She barely recognized herself nowadays. Before all the bad stuff happened, she was a bit plump, but now, she was almost all angles. Her cheekbones stood out and her green eyes no longer smiled back at her. She wondered if the old Jolly would ever be allowed to come back to the surface.

The towel wasn't covering much, but it'd have to do until she woke up from the nap she planned. The shorts and tank from last night were in the trash, and that was the only thing she had to sleep in. She was bent over by the bed, sticking her leg into a clean pair of panties when the bedroom door opened, and Knight walked in with a plate of food and a mug of coffee.

She regretted not having her gun close enough so she could shoot the annoying bastard. He'd gotten the full moon and stars peep show, and she wanted to scream at him to get the hell out of her room. Wasting her breath on the gawking asshole would be too much effort.

Jolly finished pulling the bikini cut panties up over her butt, and slid into the bed between the covers. When she finally looked at Knight, she felt a tiny spark of pride come alive deep inside. He just stood rooted in place with his offering of nourishment and hot coffee. *Ha, take that, asshole, that's what you get for walking into a woman's bedroom unannounced.* "Is that for me, or have you changed tactics, instead of beating on a door, you plan to tease me with food?"

He swallowed the drool pooling in his mouth from the sight of her naked ass bent over with one leg raised like that. It had been three days since he'd had sex of any form, but the sight of her hairless snatch and the seam of her ass gave him an automatic hard-on.

That was a novelty in itself. It'd happened a few times since high school, but not in recent memory, now it was happening again. He controlled his cock, not the other way around. He was going to have to watch himself or become a pitiful bastard like Georgie.

"I thought you might be hungry, and brought a peace offering to keep you from shooting me." He smiled at her and advanced to the bed. She sat up, clutching the sheet to her surprisingly plump breasts, and tucked the sheet under her arms, before reaching for the plate. "I owe you an apology, and I want you to know I mean it. Gladys has been a good friend over the years, and her husband, Ralph, who decided to take the early retirement road and died a few months ago. He was an odd fucker, but they seemed to get along fine, his death left her alone out here.

"When you called, I panicked, and you were standing in the doorway covered in blood after just telling me that Gladys was in trouble." She had the fork halfway to her mouth and nodded her head when he explained the situation from his perspective.

"And, you have no idea how hard you slammed me and Show's ego when we saw old Dorsey trussed up like that. We've been hunting that motherfucker for months, and there you were with our trophy all neat and wrapped up for us." She finished the food on the plate and he took it from her hands setting it on the small nightstand. "I should have kissed you right then instead of scaring you. Georgie has an excuse for his behavior, he's had it bad for Gladys for years now. Me, I have no good excuse for scaring you like that, so I apologize." He handed her the mug of cooled down coffee.

"Okay, I get the picture, I wasn't very subtle when I called you the last time, but I was desperate to get help. That man broke the window and came in, and started destroying things. When he saw me, he came after me and I, well, I shot him. I wanted to kill him, but I was sure he was the one Gladys went out to look for, and I wanted her to decide what to do with him. I should have killed him. Now he'll get out of jail, and probably come back here for revenge." She finished the last dregs in the mug and handed it to him before sliding down in the bed. She was so tired, she needed to sleep, and if he was going to be around, at least she didn't have to worry about being alone and vulnerable while she rested. "Lock the door when you leave please." She shut her eyes, willing the fog of sleep to come over her.

53

Instead, she felt the bed shift. Her eyes opened wide to see him taking off his boots and leather vest.

Knight saw her mouth open and the narrowing of her eyes, but he shook his head at her. "I'm just going to hold you until you go to sleep. In spite of the fact that seeing you standing in the doorway like some warrior princess that's been through a bloody battle and still lived to tell the tale, made me hard as a rock. I can control myself, and you look like you need a cuddle. I know I need one. Scoot over..."

She found herself scooting. "I don't need—" but his lips touched hers in the softest kiss she'd ever experienced.

His, "Shhhsh, just go to sleep," was the last thing she heard for the next five hours.

It'd been awhile since he'd stayed with a woman while she slept. In fact he couldn't remember staying or allowing his sex partner to sleep in the same bed with him ever. It wasn't a big deal, but still. Once she'd cleaned up, he could see she was quite pretty. His original thought that she was too skinny was confirmed when he walked into the room. Even her collarbones stuck up prominently and those big green eyes were stark against her white skin. He picked up her hand and held it in the palm of his. Nothing but bones covered in skin. Her wrist was so delicate it was hard to believe she was holding a Walther P99 on them earlier. The gun she'd kept in her hand was not a typical woman's protection piece, it was heavy and built more for a man's hand.

The more he thought about it, the more she reminded him of the refugees he'd seen overseas.

Was she in trouble? Or just down on her luck, and why did it matter to him?

*****

Future knew Hugh was up to something when they got to the clubhouse. He was acting so happy that it caused her to eye him like a bug on a pin. He just laughed and told her the boys had a surprise for her.

He'd wound a bandana up and tied it around her head so she couldn't see what he was going to show her before he was ready for her to see it, and carried her down the stairs into the basement of the club. She'd been there once before, so she knew where he took her.

"Okay, babe, you remember how I promised you I'd do my damndest to make your every wish come true?" Someone stuck a baseball bat into her hand and her husband took the makeshift blindfold off her eyes. She blinked several times and looked around. Show still hung onto the shaft of the bat that her hand held, and he grinned at her. Seth was standing in front of someone, and Big D smiled at her before he nodded Seth's way. The bald man stepped aside and she saw the gift the men had brought her.

The sight of Dorsey standing in front of her was too much to resist. Within seconds, she snatched the bat in from Show's hand, and was in striking distance of her prey. Dorsey screamed loud and long as she finally got her revenge. Big D had to pry her fingers from the bat, and he wiped the tears that ran down her face from the emotions her actions had unleashed. They were cleansing tears, not sorrow. He led her back to the stairs, and she heard the scream that was cut short, and replaced with a solid thunk sound. She didn't look back, she didn't care what happened to the fucker. The threat was now eliminated.

She gave Big Dog a look that let him know he was getting a little something extra tonight. He grinned back at her, he sure did like those 'extras'. He rubbed his chest in remembrance, unless he missed his guess, one of those private thank you sessions was how she ended up pregnant. Who knew that antibiotics and birth control pills didn't play nice together? He damn sure had no idea, and from the way Future slugged him when she found out, he doubted she had any idea either. Whatever she planned, he was ready for it. It took everything he had not to rub his hands together in anticipation.

CHAPTER SIX

Knight woke before his sleeping companion, and eased out of the bed. He snugged the pillow he'd been using under the arm that'd been thrown over his chest while she slept. It was strange, this feeling inside of his chest. Why should he care if she woke when he left? Hell if he stayed, she might get more than she was promised when he crawled in beside her earlier. His cock was painfully hard, and he took a few extra minutes in the shower before he put the same clothing he wore yesterday on his damp body.

He went into the kitchen and called the crib to find out about Demon, Gladys, and the good Samaritan. It was still dark outside, but someone should be around. The phone rang ten times before a sleepy Pinky answered the line. "They celebrated last night, I wasn't feeling very good and was in bed when it all went down, so I don't know anything. I can have someone call you if you want. The only body moving besides me is Tinkerbelle and she's holding up the wall until it stays in one place. I missed a hell of a party." Knight shook his head slowly. Give a club a happy Prez and his old lady, and everyone parties.

It was barely seven a.m., but the hospital gave him information about Demon since he was listed as next of kin on his ID. Demon had lost a lot of blood, blah, blah. He was resting. The doctor would be making his rounds at eight thirty this morning.

He made a pot of coffee, and took a cup to the back porch. The air was still crisp, but the sun would soon heat the world, and chase away the chill. He watched the wildlife, and wondered how long a man like him could stay in a place like this without needing to move on. The peace here was unbelievable, too quiet really. In his experience, when things got too quiet, it was time to move, or be caught in the crosshairs.

He heard noise in the kitchen and knew she was going to be a problem. She'd reminded him of a starving Chihuahua, delicate, but ready to chew your hand off if you got too close. Where she came from might give him a clue to the kind of trouble she was in, but he knew she wouldn't volunteer any information. He also knew that if she was thinking of using Gladys to feather her nest Georgie wouldn't hesitate to remove what he considered a threat to his ladylove.

Knight watched her step through the door leading out to the porch where he sat. "Good morning." It was a few seconds before she answered him with the same greeting. She hadn't moved and he wasn't going to play the gentleman and stand up to invite her to sit with him. He waved to the chair next to him, and waited for her to decide if she would sit, or run back into the house. He felt a small amount of satisfaction when she sat in the designated chair. She was cradling a mug of coffee and she wouldn't look his way.

"It's so peaceful out here I'd be hard pressed to leave this spot if it was my home." She didn't know what made her say that, but it was better than sitting in an uncomfortable silence. "Have you heard anything about Gladys? How's she doing? She hired me to help with the summer vacationers, but I have no idea what needs to be done to prepare for them."

He considered her words. Yeah, Gladys probably needed help this summer. "I'll tell you what, visiting hours are after nine, if you want I can take you to see her and she can clear up any questions you might have. I'm not sure Georgie will let you in, but I'll pull him into Demon's room for a bit so you can talk to her if he's being his normal charming self." He looked at her face and she nodded her head. "You need to believe that we take care of our own around here. If someone's fucking with Gladys, they're fucking with the Bastards, and we don't forgive or forget." She didn't flinch at his words, her head did come up, and she kept her eyes on his face while he spoke.

"You think I'm here to use her?" She nodded at her own question. "I guess I can't blame you for that. Truth is my car ran out of gas up on the highway late yesterday afternoon. I walked up here and Gladys called a garage to come with gas, so I could make it to town. I'm not exactly sure what was going on, but the man never showed. So we used the gas for the lawnmower to get the car here. It's in the garage. So you don't have to ferry me around. Just show me which way town is, and I can find my way. Anyway, we talked, and Gladys offered me a job. Since I need one, I accepted." She looked directly into his eyes. "I swear I'm not after anything here but a job and the friendship of a wonderful woman. That's it, nothing more, nothing less."

He believed her, she might be what she said she was, but he knew there was more to her story. Now wasn't the time for him to grill her though. He'd be watching her, and if she did anything underhanded, he'd help Georgie run her out of the county the hard way. He was known for his patience, her story would flesh out sooner than later, until then, she was suspect.

"Go get ready, we'll leave as soon as you're done doing whatever women do to visit the hospital." She nodded and went into the house.

She was at the door in less than ten minutes. He saw the clean face, brushed hair and her green eyes emphasized by the darkness of her eyelashes and pale skin. Her hair was almost to her shoulders in spots. He was no expert in women's fashions, but her hair looked like it needed serious attention from a professional. The simple red t-shirt made her skin appear almost pink. Her jeans were baggy and did nothing to entice a man's eyes. Why his prick seemed interested was a puzzle. He liked a woman with more flesh than bones. Didn't matter really, he didn't have time to seduce her right now anyway. He needed to see his best friend, and get the mystery of... "What's your name? I can make up one, but you wouldn't like it, and I keep calling you 'Woman' every time I need to say something."

She didn't say anything for a long minute while he backed the powerful bike from the porch steps, and waited for her to mount up behind him.

"My name is Jolly, yes, like the giant, and Santa Claus. I've already heard the jokes, so feel free to use them if it makes you happy." She didn't bother to argue about getting on the bike before hopping on. She'd always wanted to ride on one, but never had the opportunity until now.

The last two years of her life had certainly been an education. She thought she knew about the seedier side of life from working at the strip club. Since she'd left, she knew about being homeless, how to steal to survive, and if someone had told her she would be forced to kill a man, she would have told them they were nuts. The people she'd met along her journey were from almost every walk of life, and she knew that everything and person had a price. Right now, she had eighty dollars to her name and two pairs of jeans that were barely clinging to her trimmed down ass. She needed this job, and she really needed a friend. She had to keep thinking it would work out for the good. If not, she might as well head back to the club and let Porter and his goon do their worst.

She clung to Knight's waist as they sped down the country roads. The man had a thing for speed, and she liked it. She held on and leaned with the bike in the wicked curves of the road, almost screaming when he passed a garbage truck even though a semi-truck was clearly visible heading their way in the opposite lane. He laughed when the truck driver laid on his air horns. He got a pinch on his skin where the wind was blowing his shirt up. She wasn't ready to die just because she was riding on a biker's hog.

They stopped at a small diner for breakfast. He laughed at her complaint about the semi, "Baby, I've been riding since my old man strapped me to his waist when I was old enough to sit up straight. The only way I would have misjudged that pass is if you were riding my cock as we went down the road. That might have caused a problem in my timing. Don't get any ideas about that either, it ain't as easy or as comfortable for any one fucking on wheels. You're better off pulling over and I'd lay you out over the tank. Demon prefers bending a bitch over the seat. I'm a tit man, so yeah, I like my toys lined up where I can reach them." He laughed out loud at the look of shock on her face.

"Damn, for a woman named Jolly, you don't seem to have much of a sense of humor, do you? I was fucking with you, I don't screw whatever shows up for me to use you know, I'm cheap but not as easy as you probably think." He grinned as she arched a brow at him and shook her head.

"I've put my life in the hands of a crazy man. Don't drive off with strangers they said, and I had to be almost twenty-five years old before I found out they were right. I am a bad girl." She smiled and walked into the eatery.

He was so ready to tell her that naughty girls got spanked, but he wasn't sure she'd been flirting with him, or was just trying to be funny. Her smile had a suggestive look, but he wasn't falling into that trap, at least not until he knew who and what he was dealing with a lot better.

He wanted to reach out and smack her ass when she ordered coffee and toast. "I want the big breakfast special, and add a glass of OJ to that. The lady will have the same."

The waitress left and Jolly wanted to walk out and let him eat all of that food. It'd been months since she'd eaten half of what he'd ordered for her. She told herself to suck it up and eat what she could, she'd send the rest back, or maybe the bossy giant could toss it down his gullet. She'd run low on money too many times to indulge her appetite enough to have leftover food going to waste. She learned to make a small pizza last two days when she was low on funds, even stealing apples and melons from farmer's fields many times. Especially during the times she was on the road attempting to avoid James. Why her brain was dragging all of this up now was beyond her. She excused herself for a few minutes to calm her emotions.

By the time she came back, the entire table was piled with plates of food and Knight was doing his best to chew his way through it all. She ate as much as she could without making herself sick. Every time she picked up a slice of toast, he took it from her fingers and replaced it with a slice of bacon or sausage link. It was annoying and it pissed her off. "I think I told you I'm almost twenty-five years old, right? I like toast, and I'm grateful for the meal, but I'll never eat a soft egg yolk voluntarily. They ooze, and feel slimy on my tongue," she shook her head no, "I can't do it."

"I like bacon, I like sausage and pancakes too, but I can't eat another bite." His eyes narrowed at her, but he didn't argue. He finished his breakfast and sat back in the bench seat.

63

"This is what I see when I look at you, I see a pretty woman that's starving herself to death. Your nerves are shot, your skin's in bad shape, and if you were my old lady, you'd have to add weight, not starve yourself into a size nothing. That's what I see, what I feel is a different story.

"You've been running from something or someone for a while, I doubt you're willingly starving yourself, but instead of standing on a corner or stripping in a club, you'd rather go hungry. You know how to use a gun, and you're desperate for human contact. Even if it's a widow that needs help with a campground. It probably suits you just fine, because you can hide out there and save some money, before your boogey man finds you again."

He drained the tall glass of juice and stood reaching for his wallet. He saw her hand go to her back pocket to get her money out, and he gave her the meanest look she'd seen from him yet. She held out her hands and walked toward the door.

Pick your battles, Jolly, it's just breakfast. She didn't want to think of how close Knight's observations had been. He was almost dead on. Thankfully he didn't know who was chasing her, or he'd probably try to turn her over for a reward or something. Wasn't that part of what bike gangs did? When they saw the guy on the floor they said they'd been hunting him for a while.

Whatever she did, it'd probably be a good idea to avoid the members of this gang, just in case they weren't as friendly as Knight was trying to be. He was already suspicious, keeping a low profile was her best course of action.

She rode to the hospital in silence. He seemed to prefer she keep quiet, and she, well, she was going to have to wait and see what Gladys had to say, providing the woman was awake.

Georgie was sitting in a chair next to the bed Gladys was lying in. He was sleeping, and she was smiling at his snores. Jolly went to the opposite side of the bed and leaned close so the two women could talk without waking up sleeping grouchy. Jolly held a hand over her mouth to keep from laughing aloud when Gladys called him that.

"The shoulder's just bruised and so are the muscles in my calf. Actually my shoulder was dislocated, and they popped it back in, but there will be soreness and bruising. I fell out of the damned tree when my foot landed on a dead branch, it gave away, and I landed hard. I'll be fine in a couple of days, and they're letting me go around noon, so I'll be back home sometime today. We can make plans when I get there."

Jolly told her what happened last night with the biker and she whispered as low as possible when she talked about Knight. "He's an arrogant ass that thinks his threats will intimidate me."

Gladys gave her a grin. "Yeah, he's arrogant, but his looks make up for some of those bad traits. I have to tell you, I'd trust him at my back any day."

"I don't care how good looking he is, I don't trust him, I can't let myself get involved with a man like him, or anyone else. You understand right?" She glanced at the snoring Georgie, and back to

Gladys. "What's an outsider's life worth to them? Can you swear to me that if the price was right, they wouldn't sell me out?" She looked out the window so she wouldn't start crying. Why was she such an emotional wreck right now, everything was making her cry and she wasn't happy about it. "Everyone has a price, Gladys, the reward can be anything from money to power or even love. They're a gang, the only loyalty they have is for their own. If you're not one of them, you are fodder, and I'm not willing to be their paycheck."

She exchanged a long look with Gladys, they both knew she was right. Gladys knew she had a certain clout with the Bastards, but what if old enemies happened to show up and recognize her from the past. If the price was high enough, would they sell her out? She looked at Georgie, would he? The thought that he might be willing to turn her over to someone with an old grudge against her was breaking her heart. She wanted to believe he'd fight for her, but if his brothers in the club gave the order, she knew she was as good as dead. She nodded to show Jolly she understood. The words refused to leave her lips, but the reality was hard to accept.

Jolly used her normal voice to talk with her friend for the next few minutes. Georgie snorted and began to stretch. He was a big beast, and she remembered the way he threatened her last night, sending her fleeing into that closet. She told Gladys she would see her at the campground later today, and left the room. She didn't want to be looked at like she was dogshit under his feet again, so she went back to the parking lot and sat on the cement curb under a shade tree about fifty feet from Knight's bike.

After checking the expensive diamond and gold watch on her wrist for the third time, she got up and stretched. There was a small strip mall across the road from the hospital parking lot, so she dodged traffic and began exploring the shops. There was a pawnshop in the lineup of stores, and she looked at the watch again. The door handle was in her hand and before she could change her mind she went inside. The man behind the counter tried to talk the price down and told her the diamonds were fake. She told him he was full of shit, and the grey-haired older man stared at her for a minute before grinning, and nodding his head.

"Okay, so you know what you have here, so how much is it worth to you? Since you know what it is, you should know that it's worth more than I'll ever give you to pawn it."

"I know it's expensive, and I know you're a pawnshop. I won't come back for it. It was a gift from a rat bastard, and I never want to see it again. That doesn't mean I'll give it away either."

She walked out of the shop with a wad of cash and a new friend. She stopped at the coffee shop and splurged on a small frappe, before going back to her perch on the curb.

*****

Demon was in a pissy mood, he was higher than shit, and wasn't speaking politely to the middle aged nurse when Knight walked into the room. She told him that he didn't have anything she hadn't seen before, and he laughed at her.

67

"Lady, my prick is probably enough to make you faint, just give me the washcloth and I'll wash it myself, and since you're being nice, I'll wash my own balls too." He smiled at her and she was turning pink in the cheeks. He winked at her, and Knight had to laugh.

"Don't mind him, his ego is legendary. You might as well let him wash himself and save yourself the trouble of arguing with him. Truth is he's shy and women chase him for some mysterious reason. I don't see it myself, we all know I'm better looking.

Demon was laughing, "You just keep telling yourself that, asshole. Hey did you meet my nurse? She's a hot cougar, and she wants to see my dick." He looked sideways at the pretty nurse and winked at her again.

Knight had to admire the woman, she stepped up to the bed and pulled the sheet off Demon. "Okay, handsome, roll over, I really don't care about the size of your penis you know, and you might want to ask your friend to step out of the room for a while." She busied herself with several items on a rolling cart.

Knight saw a bottle of liquid with a nozzle she was screwing down on top, and lost it. He laughed until he was propped against the wall behind him to keep from falling. He kept pointing at Demon and cracking up. He couldn't say a coherent word, so he ran to the door. The sound of, "Oh fuck no, you ain't doing that," sent Knight back into gales of laughter. The few people in the hallway hearing his laughter smiled, wondering what was so funny.

Seeing the big man sitting on the floor with his back propped against the wall while he tried to control himself was an unusual sight in the hospital, especially a big handsome biker type. When the nurse finally came out of the room, she had a smug smile on her face.

He felt bad for his friend, he really did, but that wouldn't stop him from busting his balls about getting an enema from a motherly nurse. This was going to be fun. He looked around the door before walking back into the room. Demon refused to look his way until he started talking about Dorsey and his downfall.

"Hand to God, brother, I walked in behind Georgie and thought about shooting the woman, she looked like one of those Zombie things you like to watch in movies. She had blood drying on her skin and not a drop of it belonged to her. She was standing there, hair wild like it might look after a good fuck session, she had a Walther P99 in her hand, and my dick got hard. You gotta know I enjoyed the sight of a bloody zombie bitch threatening Georgie with that Walther.

CHAPTER SEVEN

Demon didn't believe him, "You're so full of shit, man, seriously, it's a good picture you paint for me though." There was no way Georgie would let a split tail threaten him with a gun or anything else. He was painfully old school about a woman's place, and not one of them would be holding a gun on him.

"I know you're fucked up on painkillers, but I swear it happened. Georgie was more worried about Gladys than the woman with the gun. He walked right up to her and she got scared, ran into a closet, and stayed there all night. He even ignored Dorsey lying on the floor all trussed up like a Christmas turkey.

"Big Dog came in and talked her out of the closet, and yeah, not my most shining moment. I saw her and, hell I don't know, it's a clusterfuck. I'll bring her by tomorrow and you can meet her. She's running from something, and not talking about it."

Demon wasn't listening, the big redhead was asleep. *Well hell.*

Knight stopped by Gladys's room on his way out of the hospital and stopped in his tracks before he reached the closed door. The shouting coming from inside the room was entertaining some of the nurses, but a security guard was reaching for the door. Knight walked into the room behind the guard.

"You don't want a woman, you want a doormat. I won't tell you a damned thing, so just leave, you

70

are unbelievable, who do you think you are? My daddy's been dead ten years now. I don't need a substitute. If I had my gun I'd shoot your big ass. Tell me what I can and can't do, fuck you, George." She spied the two intruders and actually bared her teeth at them. "Get him out of here before I strangle him with an IV tube."

Gladys pointed her finger at Knight, "You, you take Jolly back to the campground and have her bring her car to pick me up." She held up her hand when George started to speak. "I have nothing to say to you, I appreciate what you did for me, but I will never play at being a beaten down 'yes Master' type of woman, I am as good as you, and won't be treated like I have no brains. Get out, you're giving me a headache." Georgie wasn't moving and she arched her brow at him. "Okay, you want to be an asshole? I'll show you an asshole."

She reached for the phone beside the bed and dialed a number. "Hi, sweetie, can you come pick me up at the Hospital? I might have a friend with me, you're gonna love her, she's the one that caught your rat last night." She held the phone away from her ear to keep her eardrum from being broken at the scream from the other end of the line.

Georgie shook his head and left the room. The security guard followed him from the room. Knight stayed until the call was completed.

"You know he's in love with you right? Finding you laid out on that rock last night scared the hell out of him. He's a good man, be sure you know what you're throwing away here, lady."

Gladys was barely holding her shit together and didn't need to have him giving her a guilt trip right now. "A good man? Yes, he's a good man, a good man to have at your back, especially if he's backing up one of his Bastards brothers. You say he loves me, but what he said to me wasn't love words. He told me that he was going to beat my ass if he ever saw another gun in my hand that he didn't put there. My place is in my house where I'll be safe and he'll do the protection thing. Do you know something? I'm forty-one years old and never, not once, have I been treated with so little respect, even in the Middle East. So fuck him very much, I don't need his version of love."

She gathered her clothing to change, "Would you ask Jolly to come up here please? Future is picking us up and we won't be bothering you or the club again if I can help it."

He stared at her wondering what to say to make her understand. She ignored him, and went into the bathroom.

He made his way down the hallway and saw a pretty brunette that reminded him of the woman brought in with Demon last night.

Barbara Collier's room was in ICU. They refused to allow him to see her, but when he saw the kid sitting in the waiting room with an older woman, the little boy was too recognizable to ignore. One of the brothers had some explaining to do. There was a rule the club adhered to, and it was that you never abandoned your kid. This kid looked to be about five or so, and Knight knew that it was his mother lying in ICU. Barbara was the only patient in the small ward.

He left the hospital and saw Jolly sitting under the only tree in the parking lot. "Gladys asked me to tell you she needs you up in her room, she called someone to take you both back to the campground."

She stood and politely held her hand out to shake his. "Thank you for staying with me and breakfast and bringing me here."

Fuck this. He pulled her to him and laid his lips on hers, pushing his tongue inside her open lips until he had her cooperation in the kiss. He let her go and walked away.

He was halfway to the clubhouse when Future sped past him heading to town. That was another bad luck for someone story. Had anyone told Future how Dorsey came into their hands? What the hell was happening around here anyway?

*****

Knight parked in front of the building and looked at the bikes lined up. The bike he wanted to see there was parked next to Big Dog's hog. He walked in and stepped up to the bar. He downed the beer that was put in front of him and looked around the room. "I need to have a word with Fuller, got any idea where I can find him?"

"I think he's out back with Big D. They said something about looking at plans for a new place in town. How's Demon?"

"Demon is flying high on the painkillers and his nurse has his number, she'll keep his big ass in line." He grinned and took another beer to go.

73

Big D and Show were sitting on a weathered picnic table talking with Fuller and Needles. Fuller wasn't as big as the rest of the men at the table but he was well liked. Knight stared at him to make sure he wasn't thinking wrong about the kid. There was no doubt in his mind now.

After the greetings were taken care of, and he gave his report on Demon and his evil nurse, he brought up the good Samaritan's name.

"Do any of you know Barbara Collier? She's the woman that stopped to help Demon, and got ran over for her trouble. Her car's sitting at Joey's junkyard. It's pretty much totaled. Not that is was much to begin with, but I was thinking maybe someone should donate a vehicle for her if she lives. She's still in ICU, and they refused to tell me anything."

Big D was looking at him strangely, the man knew him too well. He knew something was about to go down, and Knight nodded his head at the unspoken question. "Hey, Fuller, do you have family around these parts?"

Fuller shook his head, "Nope, no one. My people are from Oregon."

Knight asked again if anyone knew a woman named Barbara. Fuller looked puzzled but walked away from the conversation.

"I hate it when shit like this happens, the boy better step up and be a man. Wait until Demon finds out he's been fuckin' that girl over, he'll know what an ass whippin' really is. He's lyin' about not knowing the kid is his. He's just being a pansy motherfucker."

74

Georgie came stomping outside carrying four beers with him. *Yeah*, Knight thought, *this day just gets better and better*.

*****

Future drove up at the hospital entrance just as they rolled Gladys out through the front doors of the hospital. The low growl of the 440 under the hood echoed against the windows of the building. Gladys was in a hurry to leave and she wasted no time getting her ass in the passenger seat and pulling the lap belt over to click it in place for the benefit of the nurse who was watching. Jolly slid into the backseat when Future moved the backrest for access, so she could get in.

"How did you talk Big D into letting you bring the Charger? I thought this car was sacred and would only start and drive down the road for the big strong man of the house. Didn't you tell me he said this baby was too many horses for a woman to handle all at once or some horseshit like that?" Gladys was still in a foul mood, but since she was taking a few potshots at Big D's ego, she felt justified.

Future laughed, "Yeah, well, he wasn't around for me to ask, so he's just going to have to deal right? We can eat at your house, if that works for you girls."

She looked into the rearview mirror and saw Jolly looking at her. "I'm Future."

Jolly nodded and sat back in the seat. She felt like Alice just landing at the bottom of the rabbit's hole. If she didn't know better, she would be looking for the Mad Hatter to show up at any time.

The drive to the campground was exciting. Future's foot found the gas pedal and didn't seem to let up at all until they pulled into the gravel driveway. It was the first time Jolly had ridden in a real muscle car and she liked it, maybe a little too much. She loved driving, and she would have given a pint of blood to be allowed to drive the beautifully restored '69 Charger.

Gladys was limping by the time they sat down to eat the huge greasy burgers and Jolly got her first taste of a real malted milkshake. "Oh lord that's good, I don't know what they put in these shakes, but it's so tasty that these might have just become my favorite food."

Gladys laughed and explained the difference was in the ingredients, "They use real malt in the smaller mom and pop places like Georgia's. No skimping on the quality of the food either."

"So, I want to hear all about last night. Tell me, was it fun to tie up Dorsey? I would have been laughing with every moan of pain he made. I would have tightened the rope as much as I could and made him scream bloody murder. No amount of pain is too much for the hell and harm he caused me. He needed to suffer."

Future wanted details, Jolly wasn't particularly fond of the memory of shooting and hog-tying the man, but she related how the "capture" went down step by step. "All I did was defend myself really. He was coming at me and reaching for the gun at his side, I felt threatened and shot him in the shoulder and in the side. I didn't want to kill him, mainly because I didn't know where Gladys was, and she seemed to want to get her hands on him pretty badly. I didn't even know his name until one of the men said it."

"When those gang members came in the door, and Georgie threatened me, I almost shot him too. I'm not real proud that I hid in the closet until some guy calling himself Mad Dog or something like that told me he was the boss of the gang and I could come out and be safe. Mostly I had to pee so badly by that time, I was ready to find a corner. I came out and the man who'd kept pounding on the door and yelling at me to come out was there. He scared me worse than the first man."

"He stayed with me last night and bought me breakfast before we went to the hospital. I'm not sure how to take a man like him, but I don't have plans to learn how." Why Future smiled at her words was puzzling, but Gladys was drooping, so Jolly helped her to her bed.

CHAPTER EIGHT

Future was waiting for her to come back to the kitchen. She wasn't smiling now, in fact she looked pissed. Jolly sat and waited for the woman to say what was on her mind. Her eyes were such a jewel blue that they reminded her of a dark sapphire.

"So, let's get a few things out of the way. You've done me and everyone around here a huge favor, so I'm going to return the favor, even if it doesn't seem like it right now. You're hiding out here, and believe me, the past has a way of catching up with us. You aren't special. It won't take long for the people you're running from to find you, this time you won't have a place to hide. I tried to see, but I can't tell you how that will end.

"The guy named Big Dog is my old man, and I'm the only one that gets to talk bad about him, so you need to remember that. As far as Georgie goes, the man's been crazy about Gladys since he saw her the first time, and from what I heard, his feelings for her have only gotten stronger. He's an asshole and he's got the mindset of a man born at the turn of the last century when it comes to women. I plan to ream him a new one as soon as I see him.

"As for Knight, you've only met the first half of the dynamic duo. Demon and he were almost cradle brothers so if a woman takes on one, she'll probably get the other one too. As far as I know they've only had one real serious fight, and that was over the most ignorant reason they could fight over." She shook her head at Jolly when she opened her mouth to deny her interest was more than it actually was. "You can deny it all you want, Knight is a gorgeous man, and Demon is a giant redhead that's more bull than man. Together, you won't stand a chance when they decide you are just what they need."

Jolly didn't know what to say, this was plain speak for sure. She wanted to ask what she meant by the prediction about the people hunting her. She was so tired of running that it might be the best thing that could happen.

"I don't know what Gladys has told you about me, but I'm pretty much resigned to the confrontation, if they kill me, then at least its over. If they want something else, I'm out of options. Gladys hired me for the summer, and I plan on working for her. I've decided to go back home to get this resolved, and then come back here. I thought about it all day, and it's been almost two and a half years of running. One thing your friend, Knight, kindly pointed out to me, and he's right about, I'm half starved, I look like a homeless bag lady, and I'm tired of running.

"As far as Knight goes, he's an asshole and I don't want anything to do with him or his friends. You might be one of the gang, but I'm a nobody, can you guarantee me some of the members of that gang wouldn't sell me out if they were offered enough money? We both know if they were hired to find me and turn me over, or kill me, they'd do it for the good of the brotherhood. I'm not stupid, all the people after me need to do is be willing to pay the price, and I'm gone."

Future heard enough, she grabbed Jolly by the shirt and pulled her from the chair. She shook her as hard as she could. "You arrogant little bitch, you don't have no idea how a MC operates. All you do is buy into the gang shit. The Bastards don't 'sell' people unless there's a damn good reason, and you think you're important enough to bother with?" Future was so mad she slapped the shit out of Jolly before she realized she'd done it. Fuck it, those men were hers, and no one talked about the Bastards like that. Not to her.

"Keep your pie hole shut when it comes to those men. You don't want them, fine, but if you let me hear from anyone that you've been spewing your shit, you'll have reason to hide." She slapped the bag of bones again, harder this time to make sure she got the point across.

Her backhanded slap caused Jolly's head to snap sideways, and if Future hadn't let go of her shirt, Jolly was going to start defending herself. It'd probably have taken everything she had, but she wouldn't stand there and be abused because she voiced her opinion.

Jolly watched the beautiful woman stomp out of the door and heard the growl of the car's engine as it disappeared into the trees. Damn, the woman had a hard slap, Jolly took a bag of mixed veggies from the freezer and propped her jaws on them while she held them in place.

When the bag became soggy and dripping, she put them in a bowl and into the fridge. She made up her mind while waiting for her jaw to stop stinging.

She'd have a talk with Gladys at dinner, and let the chips drop where they may.

She pulled burger from the freezer and made her version of a poor man's stew with the vegetables and meat. She snooped through the cupboards finding makings for baking powder biscuits and whipped up a batch. She'd just added the flour to the stew to thicken the juice into gravy when she heard Gladys moving around.

"So you want to tell me what happened after I laid down for my nap? You were smiling and opening up with Future, and now you look like someone took your happy away."

They'd eaten, and the leftovers were put away. It was odd to Jolly, the way the two of them worked so well together. She brought fresh coffee out to the screen porch, and sat down.

"Well, it's like this I guess. Future thinks the world of you, and she's the poster girl for the bikers. She told me about Knight and Demon, and their unusual attached-to-the-hip relationship. She told me about Georgie and swears the Neanderthal is in love with you." Sipping her coffee soothed her nervous system a bit. "I'm a bitch for not trusting her friends and I'd better never question or say anything about them in public or to anyone and let it get back to her."

Now was the time to bring up her plans, and hope the older woman wouldn't try to talk her out of it. She might succeed, and that'd only prolong the inevitable.

"I've decided to go back and visit my mother. While I'm there, I am going to go see Porter. You were right, you know, it's time I got my life back. Your friend, Future, said my past will catch up to me sooner than I think, and I don't want it catching up to me here where the only friend I've made in the past two years is living.

"If I don't call you in a few days, you will know what happened and can hire someone else to take on the job you've offered me. I won't come back until I can be sure I'm safe and the people around me are too."

Gladys didn't know what to say to her. Jolly had finally made up her mind and even though it was probably for the best, what if this James and his boss hurt her or worse? "I don't suppose you'll give me the name or maybe an address? That way I could send the police at the state level an anonymous tip?"

"No, I trust you, but if they knew I told someone then they might come here and hurt you anyway. I promise I'll call in three days." Seeing the look in Gladys's eyes made her want to hug the woman. Someone would care if she was dead, and that made her determined to live. "I have to stop running, and I can't wait for someone to rescue me."

*****

That night Future told Big Dog what she had discovered about Jolly. Being psychic helped at times, and she had gotten plenty from her time in close quarters with the woman. "She had the nerve to question the Bastards integrity. I should have decked her instead of just settling for slapping her a few times. I told her that Knight was a good guy, but she looked at me like I had horns or something before saying she didn't care about him or his friends, she doesn't trust him. She said that you Bastards would sell her to the people hunting her if the price was right. Like you guys would do something so horrible."

He held her close to his chest, happy she couldn't read him as easily as she could so many other people. If she knew some of the things the Bastards had done over the years, she'd be packing her bags. He let her rage, and felt her love with each word. She knew they weren't totally legit, but she defended them as if they were choir boys.

"Georgie is screwing up big time. He went all caveman shit on Gladys, and she threw him out of her hospital room. I realize I owe that friend of hers for catching my personal nightmare, but she isn't good for Gladys. She has too much baggage, and if she stays around, Gladys will need her guns back. So if you can pry them out of Georgie's hands, you might want to give them back to her."

She continued to babble about the woman, but he had heard enough, he'd take care of it tomorrow, right now, he used the only sure fire way of shutting her up that he knew. "Come over here and tell me about taking the Charger out today." She blushed as she laid on top of him. He was naked and she was about to be the same as he began to slide her nightshirt up her body.

*****

Jolly left the campground as the sun was just rising. Gladys was worried about the girl, but if it was her, she might be doing the same thing. She didn't have such a simple solution for her past or she might have left right after Jolly to deal with it.

Future drove up in her truck at noon, and Gladys wasn't exactly happy to see her for the first time since they'd met. She baked a cardboard pizza in the toaster oven and poured them each a tall glass of sweet tea.

Future wondered aloud where Gladys's houseguest was hiding.

"You know what? I love you a lot, but I'm not going to talk about Jolly right now, and definitely not with you. For a psychic, you sure got your wires crossed on that one, but that's okay, thanks to your words of encouragement, she left. That's what you wanted to happen, and it did. So what's new in your life?" The bite of pizza almost made her hurl, but she couldn't allow the look of satisfaction on Future's face get to her. The young woman had been good to her, and until Jolly showed up, they agreed on most things.

Future felt the walls Gladys had put up. She wasn't used to that from the open, normally happy Gladys. "Look, she was saying things she had no right to say about the Bastards. I just pointed out to her that I didn't appreciate her opinions."

She was going to cry before this day was done, she teared up when Jolly drove out this morning, but losing Future as a best friend was going to hurt even worse. "Really? She told you the truth as she sees it and you didn't like what she said? Rather than tell her she was wrong, and why she was wrong, you attacked her. Since when did you start being such a witch? She's right about one thing and

84

you proved it to her. If a person's not one of the Bastards, they're nothing to any of you. I'm not certain what you said exactly, and I don't want to know, but she was right. The Bastards aren't the worst MC group around, but hunting down and recovering people is one of their more lucrative businesses. If you don't want to hear the truth then shut your tender ears, young lady. Money talks and pays the bills."

Future stood and pushed her chair back with her legs. "I know the club isn't lily white, they never have been, but they wouldn't hunt down an innocent woman and hand her over for money, I don't believe you. Since that woman came here you've changed, Gladys, you don't know, you're not involved in their businesses. I'm leaving before I say something we'll both regret."

Well, that's going to be an interesting conversation she'll be having with the big guy tonight. The only way Gladys knew about the extra income the club earned in recovering people was from one of her guests here at the campground. The man had rented a cabin while he waited for his ex to be brought to him. Demon and Knight had been the ones to deliver the woman. To be fair, they stopped the man from seriously injuring the woman, but she was still roughed up good before they'd intervened. The woman slipped out of the bedroom window while the man argued with Demon, and she begged Gladys to hide her. Knight saw where she'd gone, but didn't say anything at the time. The reason she'd been hunted in the first place was to get her signature on several documents that removed her claim on property they'd purchased during a short and abusive marriage. She and Ralph made a few calls and got her away from the area, and she had the number of a good lawyer in her pocket when she was dropped off in Chelsea.

CHAPTER NINE

Demon was back to the compound three days after his close encounter with the pavement. Pinky was enjoying the way his hungry mouth ate at her pussy while she held onto his prick with both hands jacking him off. She was too short for a 69, but Knight had to give the girl credit for inventiveness. She laid over Demon's chest and was able reach her tongue just past the head of the thick cock in her grasp. Knight figured he'd do both of them a favor, and pulled a melting ice cube from the empty coke that Pinky had finished just before Demon announced he was hungry for a juicy pussy. He rubbed the melting ice on Pinky's puckered asshole and slid it inside. He followed that with two more cubes and she screamed, grinding her cunt over his buddy's face, as she came. Her mouth was opened and Demon's cum squirted from his cock being held in her death grip, hitting her tongue and face. Knight was ready to come in his pants right there.

He hooked two fingers in her snatch and used his other arm to pull her over Demon's head, leaving the top half of her hanging over his wide chest. He speared her soaked cunt with a groan. "Damn, Pink, you must've been doing those exercises again, your hole is tight as shit. Feels good." He knew he wouldn't last long, it was almost a week since he'd indulged in this favorite pastime, and watching the way she licked Demon's sperm from her lips, yeah, it was fuckin' hot. He reached down and pinched her clit, twisting it back and forth in the wetness. His hips didn't meet her ass because he bottomed out before his cock was buried inside of her tunnel. He felt her ass quivering and promised himself a trip through her backdoor next time. Right now he was ready to blow his wad and she was beginning to tighten down over his cock. He mashed her clit and shoved deeper. She screamed and his cum filled her grasping pussy. He pulled his softening cock out of her and put himself away before kissing the space between her shoulder blades. She shivered and he laughed then did it again.

He stashed a few bills in the elastic of the bra that was supporting her tits over the cups, "Buy yourself something pretty."

Demon grabbed the rest of the ice cubes from the glass and rubbed them over his face to rinse some of the pussy juice off, and pulled his t-shirt up to dry himself off. "It's good to be back." He looked at his empty beer bottle and limped to the bar.

Big Dog and Georgie were sitting together drinking and complaining about women, Demon figured he'd join them for his own entertainment. He didn't own a woman, didn't want to either. Maybe someday, but not until he found one that did more for him than make his dick hard. Not to mention the thought of sharing a woman on a permanent basis with Knight kept filtering through his brain when he thought of locking down.

"What happened to make you brothers look like you want to pound on something?" He sat and put his feet up on another chair with only a small wince. The bullet had been removed and everything was healing nicely in his thigh, but he still had to watch out and not make any moves that might pop one of the stitches.

Georgie gave him the 'eat shit and die' look and slugged back his beer. "Women are the fucking bane of every man's life. A man can kiss her royal little ass, put a ring on her finger, and give her everything he owns," he pointed his bottle toward Demon, "that's not enough for them, oh no, boy, she wants to put a motherfuckin' ring through a good man's nose and lead him around with a pretty pink fuckin' leash." He nodded for emphasis and sat back in his chair.

Big Dog nodded in agreement. "A woman is the most evil enemy a man has, yep, always getting in a man's business. She has her place in a relationship, why can't she stay in her place? Oh no, gotta snip and snap at a man. Do you know Future found out about our hunting program, I think Georgie's woman ratted us out. Fuckin' bitch." He looked at Georgie who was scowling at him for calling Gladys a bitch. "No offense to you, brother, she's a good woman with a few bad habits, like telling Future things the old ladies don't need to know." He belched and got up hitting the bar for more beer.

"Sorry, Big D, we're out of longnecks. I just tapped a keg, so hang on, it's cold. I'll bring them out to you and the guys in a couple of minutes." Big D navigated his way back to the table and swore the reason they were out of his favorite beer container was because some bitch must have fucked up something.

Needles joined the table of friends and Knight pulled another table to butt up with the one they already had. Mick, from the body shop came in, and even Beadle found his way to the table. Show sat at the bar talking to Tiny. They seemed to be the only men here that weren't bitching and whining about women.

Tiny looked up from pumping up the keg and saw the crowd at the table. He looked around and spied the bucket he used to shuffle ice from the icemaker in the back room to the bar, so he grabbed the bucket and filled it with beer from the spigot. He snagged a stack of red plastic cups on his way to the table.

Beadle's woman left him and took the kids when he came home and beat the shit out of her for refusing to let his pregnant slut move in with them. Two weeks later the slut lost the kid when he slapped her around a bit. She told him to die and she hoped bugs crawled on his rotting flesh. The bitch had given him nightmares about bugs crawling on him every time he closed his eyes now. "I don't give a damn what you say, ain't no woman worth the hell a man has to go through with one."

Demon got up to take a piss and his chair was filled within minutes. He walked past Show and shrugged his shoulders, "I got no pony in that show, and those boys are going to blame the headache in the morning on women too." He shook his head, "I think I'll just go find me a friendly housecat and give her a lap to sit on for the night."

Knight watched Demon leave the room and knew where he was headed. He was getting tired of hearing the woes of the locked down brothers as well and decided to have some fun at their expense, and really piss the whiners off.

"Well, I for one hear you all yapping and crying about how mistreated you boys are. Why don't you just toss 'em aside and be rid of them." That got some of the men's attention. "Some other sucker will come along and take what you tossed out. Fuck, man, I've seen all you fuckers' old ladies and wives. There ain't one of them a red blooded man wouldn't want to fuck, so they won't be hanging on your dicks for long." He had to bite the inside of his cheek to keep from laughing at the looks of hatred he saw on his friends' faces. Damn they were so easy to fuck with when they were drunk.

Big Dog didn't like the idea of another man talking to his woman, let alone another man taking her to his bed. "Oh fuck no, she ain't fucking no damned motherfucker but me. The first sonofabitch that touches her will be feeling my fist in his mouth before his arm stops bleeding from where I tear it off him and beat him to death with it," he mumbled. "Touch my property and I'll kill the sumbitch."

Georgie's eyes narrowed into slits as he thought about some other man sliding into place beside his Gladys and his fist hit the table, making the cups of beer jump. "I'll shoot his fuckin' balls off and drown him in that damn lake she's so in love with. Don't be getting ideas about her, she's mine, motherfuckers, and don't you forget it."

"Oh come on, think about it. You'd be free to find a woman more to your liking. There's always new sluts and party girlies coming through here.

Grab one that's still young and dumb." That got several groans from the table of men.

"I ain't got the time or patience to deal with some chickie that has trouble deciding what color nail polish matches her outfit. Damn you, Knight, you ruined a good damned bitch session for me, asshole."

"Oh hell, man, you can sell those homes you all share with the old lady, and live here with the rest of us again. If you haven't gotten used to privacy and doing your own thing, or not having to share a shitter with thirty other guys, it's great, right? Why stay in an empty house, right? Who's gonna clean it?

Beadle got up and took a swing at Knight who was trying not to laugh as the smaller man twirled around due to the momentum of a swing that had no chance of connecting. "You're a sonofabitch, trying to make me feel bad after all I been through, comme're, I'mma beat your ass. Some sumbitch is fuckin' Kelsey right now I bet, an you gotta remind me."

Knight wasn't about to lecture Beadle about the reason a woman might not want a man that not only beat her regularly, but thought nothing about moving his girlfriend into the same house his wife and kids lived in. He gave the small man a gentle push and Beadle sat on the floor staring into space.

"You get a mouse, you give her a house, and when she's gone, you don't need the house anymore. You're free agents, man." He spread his arms to his sides. "Look at me, I have no responsibilities to anyone but the Bastards and me.

I'm happy here with the Bitches, and the bar. Hell, I get pussy from a different woman each night if I want." He took a cup and dipped it into the bucket and drank it down." It's gonna be fun, having you brothers back at the crib."

The grumbles of "Oh hell no's," were music to his ears. He hated to see good people screw up their lives from petty shit. Someone busted a chair and he looked to see who was doing the damage, it was Georgie. Old boy was getting wild, and Big Dog wasn't much tamer.

They drew a man's silhouette on one of the tabletops and leaned it against the wall. It became a competition of who threw his knife in a vital spot. The "dickless motherfucker" game was on. As drunk as they were, most of them threw with decent accuracy. A heart shot got encouraging words, but the cock shot got cheers and whoops.

Needles sat with the single men enjoying the show the men with woman troubles were putting on. He saw the shit these men were going through and counted himself lucky to be without a permanent woman in his life. Show got tired and drifted off to find his bed. Needles hung in there with Tiny and helped him clean up the mess that had been made when the table was upended by a raging jealous Big Dog.

Most of the men were passed out on whatever piece of furniture they sat down on during the competition. Big Dog was laid out on the floor and Georgie was sitting in a chair with his head and shoulders on the table in front of him. Mick was in the lounge on one of the couches, and several others

93

were scattered on the rest of the furniture and in the backrooms where they'd wandered to find a bed.

Knight went out back to the shanties and kicked off his boots before lying down and sleeping. He hadn't had as much to drink as the rest of them, so the room wasn't spinning for him as he drifted to sleep.

*****

Jolly found a hotel room on the outskirts of Louisville. She didn't really want to spend the money, but if this was going to be her last night on earth, she was going to sleep in a real bed with clean sheets. She'd indulged in a chicken sandwich and her favorite caramel frappe for dinner, and sat in the hotel room watching television for the first time in months. The local news anchors must have changed since she left the area, because she didn't recognize the two people smiling as they reported on yet another murder in the basin area. It was forecast to rain all night and there was going to be more rain tomorrow with possible thunderstorms. That wasn't necessarily a bad thing for her, if the rain was falling, there'd be fewer people out and about and it'd be easier for her to visit her mother. Afterwards, she was going to the strip club to ask Porter to call off his dogs.

She took a long hot bath and scrubbed her skin with the hotel soap. The memory of the handsome biker telling her how bad she looked stayed with her. She washed her hair and used conditioner to tame the frizzed mess, but she couldn't do anything about the cut.

Sleep was eluding her, but sometime during the late show, she drifted off. The sun was up when she opened her eyes and she was startled to see it was past nine a.m.

The little coffee pot was a godsend for her jangled nerves. The hot coffee laced with three of the four sugar packets and both creamers helped her focus. She used the hotel telephone to call her mother's number since the local call was free of charge and she didn't own a cell phone. She got a recording that said the number had been changed or disconnected. *That's odd.*

She left the hotel just before checkout at eleven o'clock. Her mother should be up by now, and the club opened at three, so she could potentially spend a couple of hours with her mom and then go directly to face her fate.

She pulled into the driveway, and immediately knew something wasn't right. There was a bicycle by the front steps and rock music blared from the open windows of the house. She was stunned, her mother had moved? Why would she move, it'd only been six or seven months since she'd last spoken to her, and she didn't say a thing about moving to her then. The teenage girl that came to the door told her she didn't know anything about the lady that lived there before. She was just the babysitter. Jolly thanked her and got back in her car.

Well that was a letdown. She started the car and drove around town for an hour wondering what to do. Maybe she should wait until after she visited the strip club to hunt her mother down. *All right,*

enough of this shit, just go to the place, wait for
them to open the doors and do this.

She parked her old car on the street and watched people scurrying through the rain with their heads down, as they hurried to their destinations. She got out of the car and ran around the building through the rain and checked the back door. She looked at the parking lot and saw two vehicles there, neither was the dark blue SUV. The door opened when she turned the handle, so she went inside.

CHAPTER TEN

She heard the murmur of voices coming from Porter's office, and stood there for a minute taking a few deep breaths before tapping on the solid wood. It got quiet and someone opened the door. The man that answered was tall with wide shoulders and graying brown hair. His eyes were a green color, but it was the facial bone structure that held her attention. She could swear she'd seen him somewhere before, but had no memory of the meeting if she actually had met him.

He was smiling politely until he saw her face, now he was frowning. He stood back for her to enter the room, and she fought the urge to turn and run. Porter was sitting behind his desk with his hands tied down on the arms of his chair, and he looked at her with his head tilted sideways like he was trying to place where he knew her from. She could tell the minute he remembered who she was and he shot the tall man a look of almost, *was that fear?*

Porter jerked his head toward the door and yelled at her to, "Get the hell out of here. You've caused enough trouble around here."

"Oh no, she's not going anywhere until I get some answers, and you'd better hope those answers aren't what I suspect they're going to be." He pulled a phone out of his pocket and punched an icon before putting the phone back into his pocket. "My name's William Kelley, perhaps you've heard of me?"

She took the hand he held out and allowed him to clasp her fingers for a moment until she drew hers back. "Jolly, I'm Jolly Baker." His eyes narrowed even more as he shot Porter a you're-in-trouble-now look.

The door opened, and two men entered the room. She was thankful that neither was James. She had herself pumped up to plead with Porter to call off his dogs, but it looked like Porter might have issues of his own.

"Look, I just stopped in to ask Porter to do me a favor. I'm not here to cause anyone any trouble, really. I just need to talk to him in private for a minute and I can get out of your way, I promise." She tried to smile, but she was so nervous she knew she hadn't pulled it off when William Kelley looked at her again.

"Well now, since I'm Porter's boss, and I own this place, you can say anything you need to with me here, isn't that right, Porter? She might not understand that I already know every secret that goes on here already, so she can talk freely, right?" He was looking at Porter and the club boss shook his head.

"No, our business has nothing to do with the club, it's more of a personal problem. It's been a long time since I last saw you. We can meet later, I'll have James arrange something."

The big man moved fast and if Jolly wasn't already frightened enough, she watched him punch Porter in the mouth. "I suggest you discuss the issue here and now, or the young lady will see something she really doesn't need to be a part of. So if she needs your permission to talk, I think you might want give it to her."

Porter looked miserable, his split lip was bleeding and beginning to swell. "If you got something you want to say, say it and get the hell out of here." He closed his eyes and drew in a deep breath as if he was gearing up for more abuse. She couldn't find it in her to feel very sorry for him, maybe later if she lived through today, but right now, she came here for a reason.

"I've been running from you and James for over two years now. I came here today to ask you to stop sending him after me. Just leave me alone, I'm not talking about that night to anyone, and I swear I won't tell a soul, but you have to stop chasing me down. I can't keep a job because that blue SUV shows up within a few weeks, sometimes days." She tossed up her hands and used them to emphasize her point. "I...look at me, I've lost so much weight. I can't afford to feed myself because you won't leave me alone. I finally found the tracking thing in that watch you gave me. I treasured the damn thing. I thought it was so sweet of you to give me such a nice gift, that I kept it until I found the real reason you gave it to me. I pawned the watch off and the tracking disc is history now too. I was so stupid that I believed James was the one that wanted to kill me, but it was you all along."

She knew she was babbling, but everything came out at once, each word fighting with other words to be spoken. "If you plan to kill me then do it, if not, I want your word that you'll call off James. I'm not running anymore." She stared at his face, and then looked into William's face. "I'm not running again. I won't live that way any longer."

The door opened again, and she almost fainted when she saw the man who'd tormented her for over two years walk in. She had dreamt of him strangling her, and worse. Her hand automatically began to reach behind her where she had the .38 tucked in her waistband, but her wrist was caught before she could reach the pearl handle. William Kelley didn't say a word, he just shook his head no, and let her wrist go.

He stopped just inside the door, but advanced into the room once he'd taken inventory of the occupants. William moved aside and James laid eyes on her, his expression darkened. He headed her way, however, was stopped by one of the two men who came into the room earlier.

William turned to her and asked her what her mother's name was. "I just want to clarify something before I follow an inclination of mine. What is her name?"

"Her name's Helen, and that's another thing, she isn't living in the house we had before I was forced to run. She's either moved, or something happened to her."

"Okay, Jolly, why don't you take a walk with me and you can tell me about the past, did you say two years? I think Porter and his friend, James, need a few minutes to reflect on life and I want to hear about what you've been through. Why don't we go to that nice little restaurant on the next block where we can have a little chat." His smile was friendly and she found herself agreeing to go with him. They could walk to the place and there was plenty of witnesses to see if he ended up killing her.

The rain slowed to a light mist and it took just a few minutes to walk down the block. They sat in the furthest corner, William sitting opposite from her in the booth. He could see the door from his seat, but she was busy blowing the steam from the mug of coffee in her cold hands.

"So, Jolly, tell me what made you work for Porter to begin with? I'm interested in why a beautiful young lady like you would work in a strip club. I assume you weren't romantically involved with Porter or his henchman, so that leaves work. Right?" He smiled and she found herself smiling back. He sure was familiar, but she couldn't place him.

"I graduated from high school and wanted to go to college, but mom already worked as a waitress, and had a weekend job in a hotel cleaning rooms. I ended up working a cash register in the mall. We paid the bills, but that was as far as the paychecks went. On weekend days when I wasn't working at the mall I used to go with her and help clean the rooms so we could get home early and she could put her feet up." She remembered how Helen's feet used to swell so badly she could barely stand by the time she got home.

"Long story short, mom had blockages in her arteries and one morning she woke up and couldn't walk. I met Lisa when she was visiting her sister at the hospital and we got to talking. She said she made good money and didn't have to do anything but dance for men.

"I applied for a job, and it's strange, but Porter was looking over my application and asked me the same question you did. My mother's name. When I told him, he smiled and hired me on the spot. I thought it was strange at the time, and now I know whatever this is involves my mother in some way.

"I started pole dancing, and pretty soon mom only had to work one job. Since I could walk to work most of the time, we saved enough money for me to take some classes." She looked down. "I would have graduated last year with a Bachelors of Nursing degree." She paused as she remembered. "I stopped by Porter's office one night, to tell him that I would be quitting because I was planning to get a job as a certified licensed Massage Therapist, and I heard something I shouldn't have. The security cameras caught me and they found out I was there that night." She finished telling her tale of leaving her car at the airport. "I've been running ever since.

"So, now that I've spilled my guts and given you my life's story, will you tell me how my mother's involved in this? Maybe you could tell me why I should trust you not to give me to James?"

He watched the way her mouth formed words and looked her over as much as the tabletop would allow. It wasn't a sexually interested look, more like he was studying her.

"I think you saw enough at the club to know I'm not a nice man. In fact, some people believe I'm the Devil himself," he grimaced. "I thought you might have heard my name, but that must be the arrogant side of my nature believing the legend. Twenty-six years ago I was the manager of the Lovely Ladies

Strip Joint. There was a pretty dancer named Helen, and we had an affair. I won't tell you the details, but I'll take my blame. She got clingy, I got a promotion, and Porter got the Lovely Ladies.

"Two years ago, I got a big promotion and I'm the kind of manager that likes to be hands on. I've been doing some house cleaning, and while visiting one of our properties here, I saw someone I thought I knew. Turned out, she was someone I used to know. I had to charm her into talking to me, because she thought I was going to hurt her. It seems her daughter had gone missing and she suspected Porter. The one thing she didn't tell me was that she was my daughter."

His hands were balled into fists on the table. He saw her looking at them and slowly relaxed. The girl was his, any problems this might have caused were no longer an issue. He had a wife, Brenda, and three children with her. He was fond of the woman, but she'd been a pawn, a stepping stone to get where he was today.

"We could take a DNA test, but I know you're mine. You look like my oldest girl and my little sister looked just like you when she was your age. I used to call your mom Jolly because she was always laughing. The timeline works too. So that's why you were hired, why you were tracked instead of one of the other remedies. It also explains why Porter thought I wouldn't touch him when he helped himself to money that didn't belong to him. I'd put money on him believing that I could be blackmailed with exposing a long lost daughter."

On the way back to the club William told her that her mother was now living in a small condo. "She won't have to work if she doesn't want to, I'll see to it. If she's careful with her money, she can live a nice life. I'll settle some money on you too, that way you can do whatever you want with your life, go back to school and finish your degree, travel, whatever. You came along before I married Brenda, she can't bitch, and if she does, she'll regret it."

CHAPTER ELEVEN

Jolly was heading back to Prindale. She still had a hard time believing the past week. She couldn't wait to tell Gladys all about her time in Louisville, but she hoped the way Gladys had gotten off the phone with her yesterday didn't mean she had replaced her for the summer. She looked into the rearview mirror of the new Mustang she was driving, and still didn't recognize herself. The haircut was short, but it suited her features, and for the first time in years, her hair was her natural color of light brown. She still needed to gain some of the weight she'd lost, but that would come now that she could relax in one place without having to look over her shoulder and be ready to run at a minute's notice.

It was after dark when she pulled into the driveway of the campground. The lights were on in the office and in the owner's quarters. She saw two spots through the trees where she knew cabins were located, that had a hint of light shining through the evening darkness. She called Gladys to let her know she was there and she would be the one at the door. She was hauling her new blue suitcase from the trunk of the sporty vehicle when the door to the office opened and Gladys jumped the steps to greet her in a bear hug.

"I've been so worried. You need to tell me all about your visit and how did you get this car? Should we put it in the barn? Did you have to steal it?" Jolly hugged her tight and shook her head.

"No, it's safe to leave it out tonight, I'll just lock it. Oh, Gladys, I am so happy to be back here and I have so much to tell you. It's so unbelievable, you're not going to believe it."

"There are people in two cabins, but we don't have to worry about them."

They decided to meet in the comfortable living room as soon as Jolly got her things put in her room and she'd changed into boxers and a long t-shirt. Gladys had taken advantage of the few extra minutes putting on a similar outfit in a bright yellow.

They dined on cold beer and cold chicken pieces that Gladys had baked earlier in the day for lunches when she was too tired to cook a full meal. Jolly related the story of her week's adventure, leaving Gladys with a shocked expression and her mouth hanging open.

"You," she almost choked on the bite of chicken in her mouth but swallowed it down with a good swig of beer before talking coherently. "Your father is actually William Kelley? *The* William Kelley? As in mob boss William Kelly? Holy Fuck, I don't know whether to congratulate you or sympathize."

"Well, it's not like I plan to wear a sign around my neck claiming to be his daughter. Although he did pretty well when he found out that he had a daughter by a dancer he'd dropped because she was in love with him. He left before she knew about me coming, and after she found out, she was too scared to find him. He told me he wasn't nice when he told her to leave him alone."

"I didn't ask him what he did with Porter and James, but if he really is this mob boss, I hope they got what's been coming to them in the form of my favorite bitch, karma. I swear, Gladys, I was so afraid, especially when I saw Porter sitting in his fancy desk chair with his arms tied to the armrests."

She grinned, "I'm still coming to terms with the fact I actually have a father walking around. When he handed me a wad of cash and told me to go get my hair done and buy some clothes so I wouldn't scare my mother, I wanted to yell at him that he wasn't my boss. Then I felt kind of strange, I liked hearing the man claiming he was my dad, telling me to go buy something pretty, you know what I mean? As if he really was my father and he cared about me."

"Okay, but that doesn't explain why you're here, and that gorgeous car sitting is outside. Are you getting used to the high life now? Embracing it with open arms?" She grinned at the blush on her young friend's face.

"He proved to me that he paid attention when I told him about leaving my VW at the airport. Yesterday he dropped off the keys to the Mustang. He asked me where I wanted to live, and I really haven't decided. So I told him I had a job to come back to. He thought it was a good idea for me to come back and take some time to decide what I wanted to do. I also have one of those smartphones now, and he told me to leave the tracking on so he could find me if he needed to.

"I'm sorry I'm going on and on, but this is not the way I figured my running days would end. I thought I'd probably be dead, or worse, and look what happened. He even threatened to "bust my ass" if I didn't call him every couple of weeks." She knew she was crying, but she couldn't help it. Gladys came over to her and hugged her while she cried.

"What a wonderful thing to happen for you, Jolly, and I'm glad you chose to come back here. Things have been pretty quiet since you left. Future and I had a falling out, and the only people I've seen are people in the cabins."

Jolly sat up and wiped the tears from her cheeks, Gladys suggested they go to bed and talk more tomorrow.

"Now that you're here, you can come with me to the Bastards clubhouse so I can get my belt and guns back."

"Sounds like a plan to me, I'll be ready. I'll even drive you over there."

*****

Something had to be done and soon. Demon and Knight watched the Prez drink himself into a stupor again. This was the end to a very long week. Big Dog and Georgie had organized a rodeo for Saturday and using the term organized was stretching it. They wanted one, and left it up to the rest of the men and women in the club to make it work.

Knight and Demon were setting up hay bales and pinning bullseye targets on the bales for the "jousting" game. They set the course and made sure Beadle and Mick had the small but sturdy 125 cc's ready for the huge bikers to fold themselves over and on, to use as "horses" for the course. They had four six-foot long spears made from inch thick dowel stock that was shaved into blunt rounded "points", and even picked out a Bon Jovi classic to play during the game.

There were silhouettes stapled onto thick railroad ties nailed together to make a wall, for knife throwing and later target shooting with 22's. It would take a miracle for any one of them to complete the trifecta, the few that might get two games completed would then enter a circle either on the little bikes or on foot to wrestle in the mud the two men had worked hard to manufacture. Most of the time this resulted in the drunken competitors roaring into the arena as fast as the little scooters could carry their big asses, and the front tires would sink in the mire, tossing the man into the mud. Last time they'd had one of these rodeos, Butch had won, Tarzan had broken his foot, and Pressley lost a few teeth, and almost drowned in the mud.

Pinky and Harlow were in charge of eats for the rodeo, and Tiny had a couple of kegs on ice. Seth was helping shuttle the heavy pans and boxes for the women. He and Tarzan were turning all kinds of domestic now that they knew they were going to be fathers in the next few weeks.

Future was still mad at Big Dog and he was staying at the club until they worked out their problems. As far as he knew, Georgie and Gladys still hadn't spoken. Beadle's old lady had mailed him an Order of Protection and divorce papers in the same envelope with no return address.

Mick was without a woman now, his house mouse had taken off for the big city. Demon wondered if it was something in the water around the club. The females were all going crazy. Even Crazy Charlie was having woman troubles. The lady lawyer he'd been seeing wanted to change the greybeard into a respectable citizen, and that was just not going to happen. She was planning to run for a judge's seat this fall, and she had to appear to be staid and lily white. Charlie was not what anybody would call on the up and up, anybody that wanted to look into his past anyway.

He and Knight decided they'd try to get the Prez and their Sergeant at Arms clean and sober in the morning before taking Big Dog home, and dropping Georgie on Gladys's doorstep. The two would be a start. Hopefully things worked out, or this clusterfuck they'd made was going to continue.

Show helped him drop Big D into one of the back rooms to sleep it off, and Georgie told him to go fuck himself when he suggested the old man sleep it off too. They'd had to put Big D in the room by himself and lock the door, so one of the housecats didn't curl up with him. All they needed was for Future to walk in and see that. Big D would have to shoot his own dick off to make her happy if that was to happen.

Knight stretched out on the couch in the lounge and hoped he could sleep. The shanties out back were too full of snoring, farting drunks for him to get any rest there.

CHAPTER TWELVE

Jolly and Gladys were two miles from the MC club when they saw four or five bikes headed toward them from the opposite direction. The bikes were still some distance away, but they clearly saw one of the lead bikes as it veered into their lane, and one of the bikes in the rear jerked to the side, causing the rider to go flying. The remaining riders kept going for another fifty yards or so, then used both lanes to turn their bikes around. The biker in front went flying into the ditch and his machine laid on the pavement circling, until one of the other men hopped around the thing and shut it off. Gladys turned the radio off and Jolly let her foot off the gas pedal to coast closer to the bikers who were littering the road and, "Fuck, did you hear that? Gunfire, what in the hell is going on?"

They could clearly see the two uninjured bikers who had parked their bikes on the shoulder of the road go back to their companions, carrying guns in their hands.

They parked on the side of the road behind the two big machines and Gladys tried to get out of the car wanting to run to the men, but Jolly held her back. "You can't run up in the middle of a gunfight, we need to wait until we see someone walking around. I still have my guns, but they're back at the house, and won't do us much good now." She was busy craning her neck to see the surrounding countryside. She looked in the rearview mirror because she thought she heard an engine, and saw a white truck pulling out of one of the fire lanes that were cut into the deep forests in the area. She couldn't see who it was or how many people were in the truck, so she tapped Gladys to look too.

"Do you know that truck?" Gladys ignored the hand that'd settled on her shoulder and got out of the car. She followed, and wondered how Gladys's short legs could move so fast.

They were both huffing and puffing by the time they got to the men. Gladys yelled, when she saw Georgie lying on the gravel unconscious, and Show was on the phone. She knelt on her knees attempting to get him to wake up and look at her. She laid her fingers on the spot just under his jaw by his earlobe, to check his pulse. It appeared to be pumping right along. "What happened? We saw you coming our way then bikes started falling." She was looking at Show, but he couldn't answer her question. He shook his head and looked into the forest.

"No idea, I heard shots, and watched Georgie fall. Came back and saw they got Big D and Knight too. Demon is on the other side with them. I just called the cops, this is a targeted hit, away from our property, so the state boys need to know something's up. The ambulance is on its way."

She looked at the big man lying in front of her and felt such love and rage that she couldn't contain her reaction. She began pounding on his thick chest and calling him a dumbass, among other unflattering things.

Show went to his other side and pulled his wallet and weapons. He went to the other side of the road where a pretty slender woman was getting the story from Demon and a pissed off Knight. She was holding Demon's t-shirt to the bullet wound on Big D's chest while Knight surveyed his wrecked bike. Demon was cursing a blue streak.

"What the fuck? Dorsey isn't hurting anyone, that fucker isn't breathing unless he came back as a ghost who owns a high powered rifle. Who's taking potshots at us? Some blue balled motherfucker is gonna get his ass handed to him in hell." He went to help Knight with the wreckage of his beloved Triumph Trident and continued his verbal hissy fit.

She didn't know whether to laugh or throw rocks at the two big men who were almost crying over the twisted lump of metal. She couldn't help but be impressed and since she was being honest with herself, turned on by the sight of the bare chested redhead that she assumed was Demon. His chest was smooth and the nipple stud with the chain dangling from the piercing was sexy. He was a few inches taller than Knight, but they appeared to be evenly matched with the tight asses and thighs, at least as far as she could see with their jeans on. It solved the mystery of why Future had bragged about them to her. The two would be difficult for any woman to choose between.

Demon stomped back to where she sat with his President's blood coating her hand, and started searching the man's pockets, even reaching under the giant man to retrieve a .45 Sig semi auto. She didn't flinch when Demon looked at her and nodded, she returned the gesture and looked down at her patient. She didn't know what to say to the big man, and now wasn't the time to ask him to strip out of those jeans so she could see if the packaging was hiding an even better product. She shook her head, *what in the hell is wrong with you? You're up to your wrists in a stranger's blood, the sniper might have been, wait, she didn't tell the big guys about the white pick-up.*

Demon was shoving Big D's weapons into his own saddlebags when he heard her voice calling. "Oh uh, guys? I forgot to tell you something." He stood over her and the random thought that his dick would look good disappearing into that wide lipped mouth of hers, made him frown. Knight stepped up next to him.

"While we were parked back there waiting to see if any of you were moving around, a white pick-up pulled out of the two track back about a quarter of a mile. I couldn't see anything other than the color and it was one of those little trucks, not like a full sized one. Gladys saw it too."

The sirens got louder and the men standing went to the side of the road to wave the emergency vehicles down. The state police cars arrived seconds before the lumbering ambulance could be seen with the red lights flashing. Two more police cars came from the opposite direction, and she watched the sheriff's cruiser pull in behind the Mustang. The deputy got out and spoke into his shoulder mic. It was obvious he was running the plate numbers, and she wondered why. His head snapped up and he scanned the area around him before walking toward the crime scene.

Big Dog opened his eyes and closed them again, he moaned and told her to let him up. "Let me go, I need to see to the others."

"The others are all right, you've been shot, and you're bleeding like a stuck pig. If I let you up, you'll probably bleed out since I have my finger in the bullet hole to stop most of the bleeding. I'm sorry if I'm hurting you, but it's the only way to slow it down. Demon and Knight are talking to the cops and the ambulance is on its way, so everything's under control."

He licked his lips and told her, "Tell Future I love her, 'k?" The last words she got out of him before the medics came and took over his care. One of them gave her a bottle of water to rinse the worst of the blood from her hand and she was grateful for the small mercy. It didn't take long for the medics to load up the injured men and left the rest of them standing around while the police got their reports and pictures. Gladys climbed in the front of the ambulance and went to the hospital with the men.

She wasn't surprised when the sheriff's deputy whose shiny identification bar gave the name T. Murphy stood in front of her and began asking questions. When he demanded to see her license and the registration for the car, she began to walk back to the shiny blue vehicle.

Demon and Show watched the deputy put his hand on the slender shoulder of the girl and they looked at each other, something wasn't right here. Unless the girl was wanted for something, the deputy had no reason to put his hands on a witness like that. They watched her shrug his hand off and saw him clamp his hand around her upper arm. She jerked away, but he kept his hold.

Knight was already headed that way, and Demon was close behind. Show interrupted the state cop and pointed toward the sheriff's deputy with the two big bikers close on his heels. "You better call Barney off before we have an incident here."

The officer shook his head and cursed under his breath. By the time he reached the other four, he was out of breath and pissed off. The bikers were standing arms folded while the deputy told them to back off, "You have no business being here while I interrogate the witness."

Jolly flinched as his fingers dug into her arm and she tried to pull away, but he was not about to let up the grip he had on her. When the state trooper asked him what he thought he was doing, Deputy T. Murphy told him to mind his own business, and the language deteriorated from there.

The local cop and Show joined the gathering and watched as the two men argued over jurisdiction. Show was too busy recording the entire thing on his phone to join the conversation with the bikers and the local officer.

During a lull in the insults, Jolly asked the state cop to, "Please make him let go, my hand is going numb." The deputy finally did something that made the state boy take him down to the ground, dragging Jolly with them, before she was loose from the grip on her muscle. He'd slapped Jolly, and called her a stupid cunt. The state cop had the deputy in cuffs before taking his sidearm and calling for backup. Knight stepped close to her and took her arm to examine the skin where it was turning a deep purple.

"What was that about? He had something planned I don't think you'd find pleasant."

Jolly shook her head, "I have no idea. He told me he wanted my license and registration on the car, but when I started to open the door to get my purse, he got mean. He kept calling me a thieving whore under his breath."

Demon was the one to reach in the vehicle and get her purse. He found the registration and insurance papers in the console. He noticed the car was registered to a William Kelley and Jolly Baker Kelley.

The deputy was livid. He started shouting the whore had stolen the car, "Just look at the registration. William Kelley owns that car, and she'd as good as dead when he catches up with her. Nobody steals from a guy like him and gets away with it." He didn't tell them he planned to turn her over to that same man, the mob boss was notorious for his generosity when someone had information that he could use.

Jolly handed the papers to the sheriff when the older man got out of his squad car. "I didn't steal it. My father gave it to me." While the sheriff ran the VIN number on the car, Jolly took the new phone out of her purse and called the man herself.

"Hi, sorry to bother you, but I have a situation here. There's a sheriff's deputy that is swearing I stole the car." She handed the phone to the state officer and sat on the hood while Demon and Knight waited to see what would happen.

The sheriff got the information back and he frowned at T. Murphy. "What made you think this here gal was lyin'?" Demon didn't hear the reply but he did see the old lawman tense and look back at Jolly with his eyebrows raised.

He looked at Jolly himself and asked her the question, "Who's your old man anyway?" She didn't answer him right away because the trooper handed the phone back to her and went to speak with the sheriff and T. Murphy.

"Hi again, like I said I am sorry to have bothered you, but... well, no he didn't exactly hurt me."

Knight said, "Bullshit, the fucker bruised your arm, if that's your father, give me the phone and I'll tell him the truth."

She narrowed her eyes at Mr. Smartass, but handed him the phone, and he walked away with it. She dropped her hands in frustration. Demon propped himself on the fender close to her thigh. She looked up at the red-haired giant and shrugged her shoulders, "You know as much about him as I do. Until this past week, I never even heard of the man."

She couldn't tell anyone about William, what would she say? "*My father is the boss of a bunch of mobsters and tough guys?*" She wasn't certain exactly what he was. All the way back to Gladys's she kept rationalizing by thinking of William as a CEO of a corporation. Technically he would be exactly that. Organized crime was a business, the movies made that clear, it's either business, or personal, you don't mix the two. She sat there on the hood of her shiny sports car, and decided that this good Samaritan crap was not worth the hassle. That deputy was in trouble. If the bikers didn't get him, her newfound daddy probably would and she wondered why the thought of the man being beaten didn't bother her like it would have two years ago.

"He handed me the keys, told me it was mine, and gave me a bunch of other stuff like the phone, and told me to call him if I had any problems. So that's the extent of my dealings with him."

Knight came back and handed her the phone, before walking to the lawmen who were gathered by the sheriff's cruiser.

William was still on the line and she apologized for bothering him yet again. He must have lost his cool because the next words coming from him were not what she expected to hear. "Little girl, the only reason I'm not on my way there is because you don't know what the press will do to you if they catch wind that I have an adult daughter. The bottom feeders will splash your name and picture all over the world and you will have nowhere to hide. Listen up and listen good. Nobody fucks with my family and gets away with it, *nobody*. My family now includes you so suck it up, Jolly, and if you see that cop sniffing around again, you call that biker I talked to earlier or me. You didn't tell me you knew those boys when you were here. They retrieved something for me a few years back, so I'm familiar with the Bastards.

"Now, get in the car and be on your way. They won't bother you again." She opened her mouth to speak, but he cut her words off with a gruff, "Be safe, little girl." The connection went dead, and she was left staring at the shiny surface of the phone in her hand.

Since Demon was sitting right next to her, he'd heard most of the conversation. "So daddy really is a badass, huh, that's so cool." He liked seeing her pale skin become a light pink as he teased her. Now that he actually paid attention to Jolly Baker Kelley, he liked what he was seeing. He heard a vehicle and looked toward the bikes up on the road, and saw Show directing the brothers to the bikes.

Knight came back with her ID and the papers for the vehicle. He walked around the Mustang and got into the passenger side. "Let's go, my bike is trashed, and I need to get back to the club. I ain't riding on Demon's bitch pad, so you get to be my chauffer today."

CHAPTER THIRTEEN

She couldn't believe that she was docilely allowing this asshole to tell her what to do. Demon stayed on the hood of the Mustang as she drove toward the wreckage. She slowed down even more when Knight told her to drop Demon off. She watched the man hop off the fender as she slowed almost to a stop. Obviously intelligence was missing from his brain. He could have broken an ankle or fallen under the wheels of her car, but he smiled and waved them on.

"So, where were you girls headed? And thank you for stopping by the way. I wasn't looking forward to riding on the back of Demon's bike. Last time that happened, he bitched all the way complaining about my fat ass, and how he was afraid the tires would pop under the added weight."

If making her laugh was his intention, he succeeded. "We were headed to your clubhouse. Gladys wanted to retrieve her property and we planned to get some groceries. I think I'm happy we hadn't been there before the shootings. I can just see how that deputy would react to seeing a weapon or two in my car." She glanced sideways at the handsome biker. "Did you call Future and tell her that her man is on his way to the hospital?"

"Show did that when he called the crib for the brothers to pick up the bikes. He said Tarzan was going to pick her up, the way she drives when she's not upset is bad enough. The woman knows two speeds, floor it and stop. She's pregnant now and we don't need to let her behind the wheel when she's worried about her old man." He gestured to the left, "You need to turn here, it's a shorter route to the hospital."

"I don't suppose you'll tell me why anyone might want to shoot at you, right? Aside from the bossy attitude, and tough guy act I mean. I told Demon the white truck came from the fire lane, but he didn't say a word to the cops, so it makes me believe you know who wants to kill you boys off."

Okay, this was news to him, he hadn't been listening when she'd talked about the truck. "I missed that part, would you mind repeating this truck thing for me?"

She did, and he closed his eyes laying his head back for a minute. She knew he was still awake from the way his fingers twitched on his thigh. "William said he knew the Bastards, did you know that?"

Traffic was getting heavier, and she didn't look to see his face before he replied, or she might have known he was lying, when he said, "Nope, must have been before my time."

She pulled into the hospital's parking lot and found a spot fairly close to the emergency entrance. She was putting her license away when Knight opened her door. He must have seen the surprise at his gallant gesture, because he laughed.

"I do have some manners, I was raised by a father that would have busted my head if I didn't open doors and treat a woman like a lady. At least until she proves I shouldn't bother to treat her any differently than one of the men. If you stick around for any length of time with the Bastards, you'll see that most of us can be courteous. Hell, even Beadle will open a door for a woman, and right now that man is one grouchy fucker."

She vaguely remembered the name. "Is that the man who refused to bring gasoline for my car?" At his nod, she sniffed, "Well why would he open a door for me, but not worry about my safety out on a deserted road after dark? That makes no sense."

They debated Beadle's attitude and treatment of women as they walked into the building, and Jolly found herself hating the abusing asshole. She wanted to send the wife a card of congratulations. "He deserves to be alone, no woman in her right mind would put up with some man beating the hell out of her whenever he has a bug in his ass. What kind of man could even call himself a man yet bring his pregnant girlfriend home and expect his abused wife to take care of her?" Knight saw Show, Demon, Mick, and Beadle sitting in the waiting room right behind Jolly. Her words were heard by everyman in the room, and one woman that was sitting on her own in a corner of the room.

He tried to let her know they had an audience, but she kept running her mouth, so he lowered his head and kissed her. He found she tasted better than he remembered, and didn't really want to let her go. When he drew back, she looked like she should look after being thoroughly kissed. Her cheeks were pink and she had a slight case of whisker burn near her mouth. He'd been attracted to her the last time they met, and wondered if he was out of his mind at the time. Now she looked and acted different, this

123

time his brain was enjoying her company too, rather than just some mysterious sexual attraction on its own. She was still too skinny for his liking, but the starving Chihuahua look was missing, and she showed more confidence in herself.

He stepped back and allowed her to enter the room first. She recognized the goth guy, Show, and Demon, who was watching another man sitting across from him. The man wasn't bad looking in a greasy working in an auto shop kind of way. His eat-shit-and-die look toward her made her hesitate to step closer, but Knight was leading her to the seat next to Demon, so she let him lead. Demon smiled at her and patted the seat so she knew where to plant her ass.

The other stranger was drop your panties gorgeous, and she wondered why she didn't find him appealing. With his looks, he should be modeling men's underwear, or something that women would buy just because he was wearing them. He was wearing paint stained jeans and a tight t-shirt that advertised Mick's Body Shop. *Tools,* she thought, *maybe he could advertise tools*. Men that looked like him were usually either gay, or too uppity for words. This one gave nothing away in his expression.

Demon grinned at her before introducing the two men. "The movie star is Mick, he runs the best body shop in the business, and the other guy you seem to have already heard about, that's Beadle. He's the best mechanic in town, just don't expect him to cut you any slack if you're a woman." He leaned closer, "Beadle has issues, don't mind his attitude."

"You've met Freakshow. If you want a tattoo, that's the man to see, his new shop downtown is almost ready to open, and I'll be getting the first tat opening day." As he spoke, Gladys and Tarzan came into the room.

Demon stood as soon as he saw who walked in, and went to take the older woman's hand. "Hey, sweet cheeks, how's Georgie?" He could see she'd been crying, but she was mad now. He wondered what happened to give her that hard look in her eye. "What's up?"

While Demon was busy talking to Gladys, Jolly looked around the room and noticed the only other occupant in the room was quietly taking pictures of the gathering of bikers with her phone. The woman didn't look at all grief stricken, or worried about a loved one in the hospital. She looked like a fanatic, the kind that used to picket the strip clubs and liquor stores back in Louisville.

Jolly leaned her head closer to Knight, who thought she wanted to be kissed again. He lowered his head, only to have his lips land on her cheek as she turned her head to speak to him quietly.

"That woman over there is taking pictures of everybody, look at her eyes. I know you men are eye candy and all, but that's not what she's taking the pictures for. I'm going to go over and talk to her for a minute, maybe she is just curious, but my guess is she's up to something more." She drew back, and Knight nodded slightly, acknowledging her observation and plan.

He sat back in his chair and folded his fingers over his stomach watching Jolly walk over to the woman. He could see what she meant about the look on the woman's face. *Oh yeah, whacko in the room.* He went to Demon and Gladys while Tarzan sat down with the other brothers. "Let's walk outside and talk, fresh air will help clear our heads." He looked over to the sitting men and jerked his head toward the door, they filed out of the room with Demon and Gladys. He spared a glance at Jolly as she spoke to the middle-aged woman, and hoped they weren't being paranoid, but he had learned over the years to trust most woman's intuition. Hell, look at Future. She was a psychic, but her pregnancy seemed to haywire her abilities and reason. Yet he would always veer on the side of caution if she told him there was danger or something was off. She might have her wires crossed at times, but she'd proven herself to him.

Once they exited the building, Knight told them what Jolly saw and was doing talking to the woman. "I think one of us should follow the woman when she leaves the hospital, just in case. Did any of you drive a four wheeler here?"

Mick and Beadle had ridden together in Beadle's rusted out Chevy half ton, so they agreed to follow the woman. Demon told them to, "Be on the lookout for a small white truck. Unless they washed it, the thing would probably be dirty if it came out of one of those fire lanes. We've had a lot of rain lately, and the mud is like fuckin' glue."

Since Big Dog, Butch, and Georgie were all out of commission, Demon was in charge until one of the top three were able to take over. He wasn't a people person at the best of times, but Gladys was a special case. Aside from the fact that she was a hell of a nice woman, and Georgie having his panties in a twist over her, he liked her.

"So let's hear about Georgie." He smiled at Gladys and she shook her head at him.

"He'll live. He has two broken bones in his left hand, a hairline fracture in his ankle, and a lump on his head the doctor's had to drain the fluid from, because it was taking up too much room in his tiny skull. The fluid was putting pressure on his brain, and even if I could hope the pressure would open his mind up a little, it was only causing him pain and possible brain damage. The stubborn fool shouldn't lose any more brain cells. They're cautiously optimistic he'll be back to being the ass we know and love soon. He's still sleeping it off, but the doctor told me it's a good thing. When he wakes up he's going to have the mother of all headaches."

Gladys was passed around the men for a hug, and even Beadle patted her on the shoulder for comfort, because her eyes had started swimming in tears while she talked about Georgie.

The only thing Tarzan heard while with Future was that Big Dog was in surgery for a punctured lung. The bullet had been removed, and they had no idea how that'd gone either. Future was in the surgical wing waiting room, and Show decided to keep her company. He had a particular fondness for their President's old lady, and everybody knew it. Big Dog knew it too, but they'd come to an understanding early on, and it was all good between them.

"Well, I'm staying with Georgie, at least for the night, so I can call if there is any change." Gladys didn't tell them she saw proof that the stubborn ass cared about her. The tattoo of a small heart with her name inside situated over his heart, right under the Burning Bastards logo was proof of his affection.

*****

"Hello, I saw you over here all by yourself and thought you looked lonely, no one should be alone in a waiting room in a hospital. It's bad enough if your loved one is hurting, but when they're in pain, or worse, you need someone to talk to or your imagination goes wild. At least that's what I imagine happens. So far I've been lucky that no one I really care about personally has been in an emergency situation." She hoped her babbling would set the woman at ease, and aside from the eye roll during her little offering of sympathy, the woman must have decided she was no threat.

"Aren't you with those bikers? I could swear I saw you with them." The snide tone when she said the words "those bikers" gave Jolly all the information she needed to start a more in depth conversation.

"Oh those people? Good God, I was just driving along this country road and saw what looked like an accident. So I stopped just like any good Samaritan should. It turned out one of the bikers was shot and another one is in a coma or something. I gave one of the men a ride here, since I was running to town anyway." Jolly tried to look shy by putting her head down a little, "He said his motorcycle was wrecked and he was so nice to me, that I gave into temptation and gave him a ride. When we got here, I decided to see how the injured men were doing."

She could see the woman was eating her story up. "My name's Jolly by the way, what's yours?"

"Oh dear, I understand, but you need to be very careful of the company you keep you know, someone might get the wrong idea and lump you with those people. I'm Violet Sanders. I've been taking a small break from my volunteer job here at the hospital. I am with the Hospitality Ladies. We're the ones that roll those carts with the paperback books and things to do to keep a patient from dying of boredom while they're with us. My ladies group from the church took over the program when the last Hospitality Lady died."

Violet looked at her watch and stood. "It was nice meeting you, young lady, remember, if you lie down with dogs, you're going to get their fleas. The Devil himself is said to be handsome, until you meet him in hell. My advice is to go home and forget about this day, and those people." She waved as she walked away.

Jolly waited a few minutes to gather her composure. The bubbling laughter that tried to escape would not be welcomed in the emergency waiting room. She finally got up and found her way to the car.

Demon and Knight were standing by a large black hog talking when she stopped about five feet from the two men. They certainly looked devilish. She had to smile about the comparison. One so dark featured and the other fiery red-haired with the three-day-old beard to match the coppery color on his head. Both men were built in extraordinary proportions, and not movie star handsome like their friend, Mick, but they held sex appeal, way too much sex appeal for her comfort.

"Are any of you people shorter than six foot tall? I swear, every time I see another of you, it's like you have a height requirement to be a member. That Beadle guy is the shortest one of you I've met."

They turned to see her and grinned. She held up a hand palm out. "Oh no you don't, save the sexy smiles for some other woman you sons of Satan. I have it on good authority that even the Devil has a handsome face until I meet him in hell." She made a show of looking Knight up and down, and twirling her finger for him to turn around. He didn't immediately comply, so she repeated the gesture, and he finally did her bidding.

"I guess I can't see them, but my dear friend, Violet Sanders, swears that if I hang with the dogs, I'll get their fleas on me. I'm not a big fan of fleas, or any bug for that matter. Since you've ridden in my car, I wanted to see if I need to have the pest people check it out." She shook her head sadly as if thinking about the need to fumigate the Mustang.

Knight's eyes narrowed at her words, and Demon began to laugh. "Are you serious? *That* was Violet Sanders? I'll be damned, sooner than later if that prune faced bible thumper has her way. She's been after the Bastards for years. She calls the law anytime she sees one of us on the road, and Crazy

Charlie almost got his head taken off with her purse one time when he stopped to help the woman change a flat tire. She called the sheriff and told him the man that changed her tire was rude to her and she wanted to file charges."

"It took maybe three minutes of talking to her to get the idea that she doesn't like your group. You're in the bad category of being "*those people*" and I should watch myself around you." She shook her head and headed for the Mustang's drivers side. "Okay, slick, hop in and I'll drop you off at your choice of locations. First I need to find out where you all have Gladys's things so they're home when she gets there."

Demon followed the blue sports car as they drove to the crib. He thought about the conversation he'd just had with Knight, and knew they would have to continue the talk later. Jolly had interrupted just when he was ready to apologize for running his mouth and betraying a confidence Knight had sworn him to secrecy over. Jealousy was an ugly fucking emotion, but it was riding him that day, and he got his just desserts when Big Dog knocked his ass into the dirt. Nothing between the two best friends had been the same since. He knew it was all his fault, but how to mend the breach eluded him.

Now it looked like they were both attracted to the same woman again. This one could get them killed if they pissed her off enough. It wouldn't really matter much if William Kelly was mad at one of the Bastards, but the man had a reputation for cutting the head from the snake's body and burning down his house with his family inside. If they

131

pursued Jolly, they could get every one of them killed, and it wouldn't be from picking them off one by one like the asshole with the sniper's rifle.

Crazy Charlie was sitting at the bar when they walked into the clubhouse. He was ripping sugar packets open and scarfing them down like a thirsty man would guzzle a beer. There was a small mountain of little paper wrappers next to him on the bar and Tiny was listening to the greybeard complain about his woman problems.

"Selma thinks she can tame this wild horse. I ain't about to wear a fucking neck tie, it don't matter how much I care about that old bitch, I ain't doin' it. She wants a pretty boy, she's looking at the wrong man. I told her that too." More sugar packets were ripped open and the old guy tilted his head back to pour the contents onto his tongue. "Telling me she wants to be a judge, and can't get elected if she has a live-in lover that looks like a biker. Shit, I told her I am a fuckin' biker, and she needs to make up her damn mind." He looked around the room as his fingers were busy shaking down the sugar in the packs and saw the three that were just inside the door.

The last time Demon had seen Charlie, shit, just the thought of his old ass swinging back and forth while he was fucking his woman in the backroom, still made him flinch. That was a memory only time could dim. If he made it to that age, he was going to take every fucking mirror out of the house so he wouldn't have to see his own saggy ass.

"The fat assed sheriff was here. He wanted us to know his deputy is going to see a psychiatrist tomorrow, and he was all kinds of apologetic. I don't know what he's talking about, but I told him I'd pass the message on. He was sure acting pissed when they wouldn't let him in the gate without a warrant."

Demon nodded, "Yeah, his deputy got out of hand and he's going to be lucky if the lady here doesn't bring a lawsuit on the sheriff's department for keeping a nutcase like Murphy on the payroll. This is Jolly Baker Kelly, she helped out at the wreck this morning."

CHAPTER FOURTEEN

Jolly looked around the room and thought it was nice enough, not the rough and rundown kind of place she'd been expecting. This could be a bar at any social club anywhere. Unless you counted the couple in the corner, there was obviously more going on there than talking. A woman was giving a bald headed scary looking man head while he drank his beer. He had a scar from his cheekbone down past the neck of his t-shirt and it wasn't a handsome or interesting scar. It looked like he'd never gotten medical attention when it happened.

Demon saw what she was looking at and grinned. At least she didn't flinch or demand to know what kind of place would allow open sexual activities like that. He couldn't be sure, but he thought she was studying Ham. The brother was fucked up, had a serious case of PTSD, and he'd earned every scar he wore. His blood brother was still over in the Middle East getting his hero on. It was probably a good thing Ham's cock was currently being serviced by Belle, or she might have walked over and asked to see it, as closely as she was watching the scarred brother. The man was called Ham for two reasons, he came home from his two tours looking like hamburger, and his dick had gotten split at the head down to his shaft. His cock loosely resembled a ball peen hammer, so Ham was his tag.

Demon didn't like the idea that Jolly was looking at another guy, regardless of why. That was odd, and he shook it off. Knight scowled when he saw what was happening, but he didn't say anything either.

"Will you try to stay put if we go looking in Georgie's room for Gladys's stuff? This is Tiny and he'll give you whatever you want to drink, we'll be back in a few."

She looked at the heavyset man on the other side of the bar and smiled. "Go ahead, I'll keep him company and give him a break if he needs one. I've tended bar before." She hopped up on a barstool and turned her back on the two men that had such frowns you'd think someone swiped their wallets.

Tiny got her the coke she asked for and smiled. "Did I hear you being called Jolly? I like it. Do you tell jokes or something?"

She had to grin. This man was friendly and seemed like a good guy. So she went with the old joke, "How do you drown a blonde? You glue a mirror to the bottom of the swimming pool." He grinned and they exchanged blonde jokes for a few minutes. Those dumb jokes led to a discussion on the possibility of zombies and the conversation got a little odd. They'd just about come to a conclusion on the possibility of walking dead people when Ham came to the bar and set the beer bottle down asking for another.

His voice was raspy and deep, it matched his looks. "Man, do you got any painkillers back there? My damn back is giving me hell today. I gotta ride to Downing's and get my mail, but I don't think my fuckin' back will hold up."

Tiny poured the man a double shot of Jack, and shook his head, "I'm out. Supposed to get more tomorrow afternoon when Billy shows. Until then this is it."

Jolly was hesitant to speak up, but the man looked to be in serious pain, and she could probably help him. "What's wrong with your back?"

Demon and Knight came into the room and saw Jolly sitting her ass on Ham's hips while she worked on the muscles and scars with her hands. She was telling him everything that she was doing, what muscles and tendons, she was manipulating each time her hands moved to a different spot. Tiny was handing her a wet towel that was steaming and she told Ham to expect heat. "The moist heat will release the muscle so I can get these knots to relax. They should have told you to find a hot tub when this happens. A whirlpool would be ideal for this if you don't have anyone to help you at home. In a pinch you can use deep vibration to make the muscles loosen up, but you would need something more powerful than your girlfriend's vibrator, you can get the good ones through mail order or on the internet."

The groans coming from Ham were weird but no one had seen the man without his back protected by a wall when inside a building before. He was almost always covered by a shirt or his cut to cover his scars too. Yet here he was, allowing someone not only behind his back, she was moving at will all over the scarred landscape and he hadn't thrown her off or killed her yet.

His hands were gripping the table near his head, and the knuckles were no longer white from straining to hold on. He allowed her to cause a small amount of pain to bring relief from the unrelenting clawing feeling he normally felt when his back tightened up like it had today. "I swear to God, lady, you've got magic hands. I can feel it letting go for the first time in over a year. Marry me." By the time she worked her way to the back of his neck and scalp, he wanted to cry, the pain had lessened so much. It was still there, but not like it was before she took pity on him and offered to help. He was going to buy a damned Jacuzzi like she said, and wallow in the fucker like a pig in mud.

She worked on the scarred warrior for over an hour. He hadn't been given instructions on how to relieve the pain from his muscles contracting. If he got massage therapy for a while, and did as she suggested, he'd learn to keep those muscles fluid and lighten his pain level immensely. He wouldn't need to live on pain meds and booze to function all of the time.

By the time she climbed down from her perch, her legs were wobbly, but she smiled at the look of gratitude from Ham. He started to roll off the table and she shook her head at him. "You need to plan your moves, you have to remember that your muscles will contract again, so keep them stretched as often as you can. I know big bad biker boys would rather someone slit your throats than admit to doing yoga, but in the privacy of your room or wherever, do some of the stretches I told you about. I promise you it will help a lot."

Demon would have pulled her off Ham when he came into the room, but Knight held him back. His quiet words stopped him mid-stride. "Look at him, he's been in pain too fuckin' long, I don't like it either, but he needs what she's doing." It made him really look at Ham, the poor bastard was clenching his teeth, but the liquid pooling in the corner of Ham's eye told him to relax. He didn't need to go apeshit over something as innocent as this. He still didn't like to see her touching another man, but there had been times he wished for a miracle cure for the man. His back would bow, or he'd be sitting with his torso twisted to the side, drinking himself into oblivion.

He stepped up and offered his hand and arm for Ham to pull himself up like Jolly was trying to show him to do. She smiled at him and he felt like she might actually like him for once. She'd been studying him since he'd laid eyes on her, this smile of hers was one he could get used to.

Jolly picked up the cold wet towels she'd used on Ham's back and walked over to the bar where Tiny was standing. "Thanks for helping me with these. I couldn't have done all of that by myself."

He grinned and nodded at her, "What's brown and red?"

She shook her head that was one she hadn't heard, or had forgotten. "A brunette that told one too many blonde jokes." She groaned and laughed.

"Okay, funny boy, you win that round. I have to get a move on. I still need to get to town and buy some groceries and get back to the campground to get clean clothing for Gladys in the morning." She picked up her purse and started for the door.

Knight caught up with her at the door. "We went through Georgie's place and couldn't find a gun belt or extra guns anywhere. If he's still got them we can't find them. Tell Gladys if she needs firepower she can come choose what she wants anytime." When she turned back to the door he grabbed her arm, "I almost forgot something." He kissed her and she was needy enough to let him, encouraged him even by opening her lips and dueling with the tongue that invaded her moist mouth. He drew back and steadied her with his hands on her shoulders, before stepping away. He smiled and walked toward Ham.

She walked to her car in a daze from the kiss. Fumbling with the key fob, she finally pressed the correct unlock button and opened the driver's side door, and slid in. Her key was in the ignition when the driver's door was opened and Demon stood there. He reached down and tilted her head sideways. Before she could say anything, his mouth found hers and she was treated to an open-mouthed fuck. They were both breathing harder by the time he let her lips loose. "You taste as good as you look." He shut the car door and patted the top. "Drive safe," was all she heard as she backed out of the parking spot.

She knew she was being stupid about the two handsome men. It wasn't a question of her being shy, or even caring what other people thought about her. Those two would make a woman as crazy as the guy with the sugar packets. He had to have eaten a half cup of sugar, *how is that even possible*? The man was wired when he stomped out the door, and said that Selma was history if she didn't accept him as he was. "I'mma free man, and I'll be damned if I stand still while she puts a choke chain around my neck." She hated to see older people in such misery, but this old guy looked like he was ready to lay down the law with his woman.

"I'll just chalk the attraction down to my being as horny as Demon and Knight are." Although how those two could possibly be horny was unthinkable. From what she observed at the clubhouse, the men had plenty of female flesh available without creating permanent strings. The lure of enjoying access to either of those men's bodies was a powerful thing. There had been hundreds of men who came into the Lovely Lady that could've tempted her out of her panties, but she hadn't wanted to become a discarded toy like so many other dancers. Like her mother appeared to have been.

If she took on one of them, she'd probably end up with both of them, according to what that nutcase psychic seemed to believe. The idea of two men sharing her had a certain appeal. Would they be forceful and bossy in the bedroom as they were in reality? "Okay, Jolly, they're sexy, they are really, really sexy, but what happens to you when they decide you're not enough, and you become the 'go to girl' between other women?" All she could do was hope the opportunity never presented itself, if it did, she feared the temptation would win.

On the bright side, a failed ménage romance might force her to decide to go back to college and finish her degree in Physical Therapy. With the number of years it would take to finish school, not to mention the internships, gaining that degree would take her into her mid-thirties. She was already a Certified Massage Therapist, but had never used the certification to work. Mainly because she wanted to be in a clinical setting or have her name associated with a real medical facility, and not some sleazy massage parlor like the one next to the Lovely Ladies. The Happy Endings massage parlor gave her the creeps. She'd seen some of the clientele that stumbled inside that storefront, no thank you.

Jolly drove around until she saw a grocery store and parked the car. Hopefully she could remember what had been on the list, but she knew Gladys would understand if she forgot something. It was the first time in years she'd pushed a cart through the aisles, or could buy anything to eat that caught her eye, and she took her time.

The cart was filled by the time she got to the checkout, and she piled as much as possible on top of the conveyer belt. She felt a little panic in the pit of her stomach when the total reached two hundred, but she swiped her shiny new charge card and waited to see what happened. The relief of seeing the register spit out the receipt was welcome and the trunk and backseat of the Mustang were full by the time she emptied the cart.

Thank you, William. On the way back to the campground, thoughts of his demands that she,

141

"Take the charge card, Jolly, and you'd better use it," filtered through her mind. She'd told him she didn't need his money, she was capable of earning her own. That little speech hadn't gone over well at all. The man asked her if she had ever had a spanking before. From the look on his face she believed he was actually considering the action. "You will take the card and use it, or I can take you to my home to meet my wife and children, and move you in. I take care of my own. Just because you weren't around when you were younger doesn't mean a damn thing to me. When people find out you're my daughter, they will kiss your little ass. You will have two bodyguards at all times, no matter where you want to go, or who you're with. It's your choice."

The idea of having a second parent still hadn't sunk in. It certainly warmed her heart to know he demanded contact with her, even if he was the kind of man that people feared and envied. She wouldn't have dared approach him, but he pulled her into his sphere, and wonderful things began to happen. *"My own fairy Godfather"*. The double meaning of Godfather, made her giggle.

*****

At Church that night, Demon was happy to see the room full of brothers. Most nights like this became rowdy and a lot of big talk happened, but tonight the room was almost silent as he related the day's happenings.

"The only clues we have aren't enough. A small white pick-up and someone who owns and is familiar with a .308 sniper's rifle. We know it's

142

either a bolt action or single shot, because it took a few seconds between rounds fired, unlike the night that asshole shot me. That guy had a .383 semi-auto. Probability says it's a lone gunman, but we don't know, and not knowing could get us killed.

"Big Dog is out of surgery and will be home by the end of the week if everything works out alright. His old lady is staying there with him for now. Georgie landed on his head, and hasn't come too yet, but Gladys is up there tonight, and we hope there's news by morning. The rodeo is cancelled until further notice, so it'll give you some extra time to practice falling in the mud, right, Pressley?"

There were some laughs, but the brothers began to offer suggestions, and some were good ideas. They decided to do tag teams in the fire lanes and check out any suspicious people who might be communing with nature with a sniper's rifle. Crazy Charlie volunteered for the first team, and shamed his old friend, Joker, into partnering up, "Show the young bloods how it's done." Show had his hunting partner, Larry, and Heckle stepped up to partner with Deago Pete. They'd search in a trident pattern and meet in the center of each area. Demon snagged Pressley to go with the greybeards as a pack mule, but waited until after Church had disbursed to tell the two old brothers about his decision.

"I don't need no fucking babysitter, and the last titty I had in my mouth sure didn't belong to my mother, so I'd say you're overstepping your bounds, Demon. I survived a hell of a lot worse than a stroll up into the hills."

143

He knew Charlie would start a fight to prove his point, but there was no time for that shit. "You think this is about you? Open your eyes, old man, that boy is as wet behind the ears as I've seen. If Tinkerbelle hadn't insisted on blowing him for Christmas, and showing him the ropes, he'd still be a virgin. I want him paired with men who've been in a firefight. You and Joker have both been in the jungles of Hell and are the only one's I'd trust not to send him off on a fucking snipe hunt. He needs to build some muscle and stamina, packing his ass up with the little bit of shit you'll take is gonna help him. If you don't want him to go with you, I'll have to have him go with that fucker, Heckle, and we'll end up having to rescue him from the forest."

Charlie stared at him for a full minute. "Why didn't you just say so? You need to learn to communicate, boy, I was about to have a throw down here with you." He muttered something that sounded like "dumbass" under his breath and stomped off.

Joker was standing to the side of the conversation considering Demon, "You know, I seem to recollect that Pressley spends most of his time in the shed pumping iron. And didn't that boy half kill the motherfucker that kicked a stray dog in town? Ain't that where he got that cur that sits like a rock under the table waiting for scraps?"

Demon refused to acknowledge Joker's observations. He shrugged and walked to the bar to grab a beer. If it wasn't for fucking snipers and feeling the need to watch out for the old bastards, he'd be on a highway heading somewhere now.

With the Prez and his circle out of commission, he was next in line to make the decisions.

He saw Fuller sitting with Vicky and Teach, and remembered the talk he'd planned to have with the little cocksucker after Knight had filled him in on the woman and kid. There were a lot of things he could tolerate in a brother, abandoning your kid and the kid's mother wasn't one of them. He pulled a chair out and sat his bulk down opposite Fuller. He barely spared a glance at the woman, his word "scram" was immediately obeyed. Even Teach left the table.

He sat for a minute staring at Fuller, trying to decide whether to throw the little fuck into a wall, or talk to him first. He wanted to beat the man bloody, but if he did that, then his immediate plans would have to wait. Fuller made to get up but was smart enough to sit his ass back down when Demon made a low growling sound in the back of his throat.

"You know, Fuller, we have a rule about treating our kids like family, we don't fuckin' hide them, and we don't fuckin' forget them. If their mommas need anything, a brother steps up and makes sure her and his kid are taken care of. The woman that stopped to help me is still lying in that hospital bed, and her kid is still sitting in that fucking waiting room with his granny. I had a long talk with the two of them while they waited for Barbara to get better. They live in a goddamned rat hole, and Barbara was on her way home from her job at the poultry plant, in a car with bald tires, burned more oil than gas, and rust was the only thing holding it together. She was damn lucky she hadn't been killed in a wreck before that fucker filled it full of holes. She also works part time at the tire place in town to make sure your kid has food and clothing to cover his little ass." His voice had only gotten louder with his prosecution of Fuller, and the man was acting outraged that he'd been called out.

The words, "It's none of your business," came out of the cocky young bastard's mouth and people all around them started getting up and pulling tables and chairs away from where Demon was rising from his seat. No money exchanged hands or bets made on this fight, everyone already knew Demon was abandoned by his own father as an infant, truth to tell probably a third of the club members had been raised in similar circumstances. Fuller would get no sympathy from any man here.

Demon grinned as he shoved the table from between him and his prey. He wanted to hurt something, and this fucker was lacking the brainpower to understand he was facing the worst ass beating he'd ever imagined. "Well now, I was really hopin' you'd be dumb enough to say something that fuckin' stupid."

Fuller knew he was screwed when the third slap landed on his ear. While Demon grinned at him, holding his shirt to keep him in place, the fist to his gut told him that he was one dumb sonofabitch. The punch to his jaw wasn't enough to knock him out, but he saw stars and the big man wasn't finished. He hadn't landed one punch, and all he wanted to do right now was let the pissed off giant kill him or knock him out, he didn't give a damn which way it went, as long as the pain stopped. He felt himself flying through the air onto a tabletop that immediately crashed to the floor, and watched as the redheaded Demon from Hell stood over him.

"That shiny Jeep you like to show off in now belongs to Barbara. The club owns a nice little block of rentals, and the one she and the kid are moving into, you," Demon took a deep breath trying to calm himself down. "You motherfucker are paying the rent for them." He pointed his finger at the prone Fuller who could barely see out of one eye. "If I find out you cause her another minute of trouble or problems, you won't be a problem for long. You got that?" The nod from a bloody lipped Fuller was enough for Demon. He went to the bar and downed a beer.

Knight talked to Needles and waved Teach over to him. "Take the fucker home, leave him fifty bucks in his wallet, take the key to the Tulip street house and give the old lady and kid the money and key, if she needs help moving anything, call Tiny."

CHAPTER FIFTEEN

Something had to give. The breach between him and Knight was like a damned canyon and if he didn't find a way to patch it up, he might as well hit the fucking highway. Membership was growing faster than anyone could have guessed it would, so there was plenty of business for him to take care of between the various chapters.

Fuck it, he was too restless to sit around here and wait for another crisis to fall on one of them. He needed to blow the cobwebs off, and there was only one way guaranteed to help with that, even if it was almost ten o'clock at night.

He was on his hog before second guessing himself, and opened the throttle the minute he got on the road, noticing there was almost no traffic.

*****

Knight finished his beer and watched Demon stride to the door. He felt the need to go after his best friend and have the talk they'd put off for too damn long. This friendly stranger attitude between them was fuckin' bullshit. The fact of the matter was that he was the one to cause the rift to begin with. If he hadn't told Demon about joining Big Dog and Future that day, there wouldn't have been a problem to begin with. They both had a fascination for the woman, and were aware of the other man's feelings at the time.

*****

Demon knew someone was following him, he could hear the growling rumble of the Harley's engine. It was too dark to see who was riding the hog, but then he didn't really give a shit. With the way things had been going around the crib, who knew what they were tracking him for. The second bike stayed a distance behind him, which pissed him off. He backed off on the throttle, and allowed the other bike to come up on him. This better not be some lame assed excuse for one of the less than ethical brothers to attempt to convince him to help stage a takeover of the club. He'd been approached a few times since Big Dog was voted in as the Chapter's President. Hell he'd enjoyed the courting, but push always came to shove and his loyalty to the club and Big Dog was the only reason he hadn't moved on long before now. Well, that, and Knight. They'd been closer than brothers most of their lives, and he wasn't ready to give the relationship up until he had to.

Something twisted in the pit of his stomach when he saw Knight on his Harley. The Triumph was now history, so the man was down to his last two bikes. The hog was one he'd helped Knight chop a few years back, and as far as he knew, hadn't been ridden since the day of the fight between them. He saw a two track ahead and knew it led to the lake next to Gladys's campgrounds. The lakeshore wasn't manicured as a beach, it was littered with driftwood and scrub plants, but it suited his purpose for stopping. He parked the bike on the hard packed ground within sight of the shore and grabbed his jacket and a pack of smokes, before walking to a spot with a log to rest his back against. Normally he'd take the time to build a fire and watch the flames for hours while he examined his thoughts.

Knight followed Demon down the dirt track and parked his hog. He sat for a minute to gather his balls and dismounted. It was way past time to clear this shit out of their lives. He reached into his saddlebag and pulled out the two bottles of Jack he'd taken from the storeroom. He would replace them later. Tonight, well tonight they were gonna get fucking shitfaced and by morning he planned to feel like gum on a sidewalk. It'd been too damn long since they'd just sat together sharing a bottle and talking.

He sat on his ass and cracked the cap off the first bottle. "Tonight, we get this shit taken care of, or we don't leave till morning, you got a problem, it gets laid out here and now. We've been friends too fucking long for all this pussy shit." He took a healthy swig and swallowed, nothing burned like Jack going down. He took another, and handed the bottle off to his silent friend. "The way I see it I shouldn't have fuckin' bragged to you about Future. Truth is they used me to prove a point. Don't get me wrong here, I knew what it was and I joined in that beautiful bitch's lesson in self-image. I knew she preferred Big D and it hit my fuckin' ego. I should have tucked my dick between my damn legs and shut the fuck up."

He grimaced and took the bottle back for another drink. "She never said a damn thing when it was over, not to me. I caught up with her the next time I saw her and she acted like she was embarrassed to be seen standing in the same room with me." He picked up the pack of small cigars and lit one. Damn but this felt good, like old times. "Big D had a little confab with me later and threatened to rip my dick off and stuff it where I wouldn't need it if I came anywhere near her again." Another drink of Jack and he blew out a lung full of smoke. "I mighta got the prize, but like any other thing, nothings free, even a ten minute ride on the Prez's old lady with his blessings. Ain't gonna lie, it was good, just not worth it."

Okay, this was half news to him. All he'd known was the one ménage between Big Dog, Future, and Knight. "All this time I thought it was just about me running my jealous mouth, I didn't know about the rest you asshole. Sonofabitch, we both fucked up and took it out on ourselves." He picked up the bottle between them and knocked back two deep swallows, before setting it back down. "I've been feelin' guilty about acting like a jealous kid with a big mouth. You got what we both wanted and the hostility to go with it. Is this what Teach is talking about when he sits on his ass all fucked up and lectures us about irony?" He lit a cigar, and sat forward, shaking as he tried not to laugh. Sputtering sounds slipped between his lips and he gave up trying to hide his laughter. He looked at Knight and couldn't stop no matter the frown on his face. "Com' on, it's as fucked up as we get in a deal like that." He laughed until he started coughing, still sitting there making little noises. "You want the real irony? When Big Dog made it known she was his property, I lost that need to fuck her. Don't get me wrong, man, I'd still give her a ride, if she hadn't locked down with him. She's still got that whatever the fuck she has. My prick just ain't begging for a go at that anymore."

"Fuck yeah, I got that too, man. She lost some of that shit, and now I got left holding the shitty end of the stick. You an' me, we don't fight over bitches, we fuck 'em." A toast with Jack was called for and he tilted the near empty bottle toward Demon before taking a couple more swallows, then passing the rest to his friend. "Drink that bitch, I got another one." That was funnier than hell, and it was his turn to laugh. "Speakin' of drinkin' bitches, it's been too damn long since we got one an' showed her how it's done."

Demon was well on his way to on his ass drunk and he knew it, right now he was just fucked up. "That's another problem, fuck, little mob daughter, I know you got the hots for her same as me. She's skinny, but she's got those big ol' green eyes, and we could always keep her tied the fuck up and feed her, remember whatserface? You know, the one that fucked up her damn jaw trying to deep throat me? I even warned her not to try, remember her? She liked to lick peanut butter 'n jelly off our pricks. I wonder if she's still around."

Knight vaguely remembered the woman. She made the rounds with the guys at the club a couple of times a month, what the fuck was her name? She used to come in all dressed up like a little girl, complete with the little girl dresses and pigtails in her hair. She called the men daddy and never refused to fuck, no matter who was ready to stick his prick inside her holes. Not that it mattered, even

152

Demon's donkey dick wouldn't be big enough for any hole on that woman by now. "That's the one ol' Heckle was fistin' last time I saw her I think," he laughed for a minute. "At least it looked like her from the rear end. Heckle was almost up to his elbow, an' he was telling her to suck ol' Virgil's cock. Damned if I don't think she and Virgil set up house."

"So what do we do about the princess? If we play with her, she could tell daddy, and you know what that means. Not that I give a shit, but that sonofabitch has a reputation, and nobody but us needs to get whacked if we're too stupid to leave her be. Even if we hit the road, he can hire another bunch like us and dead is dead. He wiped out whole fuckin' families 'cause he was pissed off at one of them."

That point to ponder was a good reason to crack open the reserved bottle and light up another cigar.

They caught up on their separate activities since they'd stopped hanging with each other and when the first fat raindrops hit their faces, they laughed. The lightning that hit on the opposite bank of the lake woke them up a little to the possibility that their spot on the lakeshore probably wasn't the wisest choice for them, and they tried to stand upright. Demon was holding Knight up as they stumbled toward the bikes. Knight was holding the bottle.

"Hey, man, its fuckin' rainin'. The fuckin' rain is gonna pool in my crotch and I hate when that happens. Didju know that one time, when I was commin back from Minni, Minnisho, damn what the hell is the name of that place? It's up north. Don't matter, I hit freezing rain, and my damn prick fuckin' disappeared. The sumbitch retreated, chicken shit motherfucker. Took me a goddamned hour to get it to come out again, had to piss so fuckin' bad. Pants was frozen."

Demon wasn't sober and he knew there was no way either of them would navigate the bikes in this rain. The way the lightning was hitting the sky and lighting it up, he wondered if they were smart to stay out of the trees. His foggy mind didn't have to consider what to do, the old oak was falling down behind the bikes before he could form words. "Fuck, dammit, of all the stupid shit." The wind was picking up speed and the rain pelted their heads and faces.

"Sonofabitch, I'm losing my damn buzz."

*****

Jolly was watching the Special Report on TV. The entire area was under a severe thunderstorm warning, with damaging winds and golf ball sized hail. There were tornado warnings and watches scattered over almost every inch of the map they were showing, and she started looking for lanterns and candles. When Gladys called before the storm began, she told her the people in the two cabins would be fine, "They have automatic generators that'll kick in when the electricity goes out."

The generator for the house was in the barn, but she wasn't sure if it would automatically kick on or not. That was something Ralph had always taken care of. The electric lines from the road were buried two years ago, so if the lines went down, it would be quicker for electricity to be restored to the campground. She located the lantern and candles right where Gladys said they would be, and put the long barreled lighter next to them. She heard the hail beginning to hit the metal roof and walked to the back door to look out into the yard and almost screamed.

The Walther was in her bedroom, but the .38 was sitting on the lamp table next to the couch, and she grabbed that to assure herself she was protected in case the two figures she saw in the light of the lightning strike were looking for more than just shelter. She heard them yelling from the balls of hail hitting them, and would have laughed if she wasn't so scared. The pounding on the screen door made here jump, and she was about to ask who they were when she heard Demon's voice yelling.

"Open the damn door, princess, we need to get under cover, this fuckin' lightning isn't fuckin' round out here."

She flipped the outside light on, and sure enough, Demon and a shivering Knight stood at the door waiting, trying to protect their heads with their raised arms. She hurried out through the kitchen door and into the porch to unhook the screen.

They rushed inside and she could see they were a muddy wet mess, and unless they were injured, they appeared to be drunk. They headed for the kitchen door and she told them to wait a minute, "You guys are not going to mess up the floors with your filthy boots. Take them off before you come inside." She pointed a finger at them. "You stay right there and I'll get some towels to put on the floor to protect them from your mud."

She could hear them talking while she made her way to the linen closet and grabbed a stack of towels, hurrying back to where she'd left them standing. When she rounded the corner into the kitchen, she stopped in her tracks. Seeing two naked men passing a bottle between them, leaning against the counter, was unusual by anyone's standards. Seeing the two shaggy haired, centerfolds naked, well that was breathtaking.

Jolly couldn't decide what she wanted to do. Laughter would have been an option, but they were doing enough of that themselves, and how she could laugh and drool at the same time was beyond her at the moment.

Knight saw her standing in the doorway, and pointed his finger at her. "See? You said no mud." He pointed to Demon, and then his own bare chest, "See? We got no more mud."

Demon was nodding his head in agreement with those wise words. "Didn't want you to shoot us. I heard you like to shoot fuckers that make a mess. I don't want to be shot again, that shit hurt like a motherfucker last time." He grinned when she handed him a towel to dry off with, before saying, "Although, if you want to hog tie me, and have your wicked way, we can negosh…" he stopped in the middle of the word he was attempting and went with, "we can talk about that."

Lightning cracked overhead, but she didn't care, her eyes were glued to the miles of male flesh begging for a woman's touch, her touch. The tips of her fingers actually itched to touch and explore every smooth muscle and pulse point she could find. She licked her lips and shook her head. She wanted to taste each line of ink decorating their flesh, learn the places on each man that would make him shiver with just the touch of a finger or her mouth. These two had been drinking, and from the looks of it, and the sounds of their carefully spoken words, she knew tonight was not the time for what her body was urging. She could feel the way her cunt was readying itself for a long awaited fuck fest. The liquids were fairly dripping from her body, soaking through her panties and the short boxers that she was wearing. She felt the lips of her pussy thickening, almost tingling in excitement. Her nipples didn't bother hiding the excitement of seeing the two men in all of their glory.

"Okay, let's get the two of you cleaned up and find a place for you to sleep for what's left of the night. Follow me unless you already know the way to the bathroom, I'll see if I can find you something to wear, and toss your clothes in the washer."

CHAPTER SIXTEEN

There wasn't one article of clothing in the house she could find to fit either man. So she handed each one a twin sized flat sheet and told them, "You boys get to dress up roman style and I'll hurry and get your clothes washed. Let's hope we don't lose power until they're dry."

Jolly hurried back to the kitchen and took the empty laundry basket off the dryer to gather the sopping wet mass of clothing. The denim vests with skulls and fire were amusing. There were several patches and small pins scattered over the material, and she wasn't sure if they should be washed with their mud soaked jeans or not. Either vest would have made a sleeveless dress on her. One would have been longer and looser on her body. She decided to hang the two on the bar made for clothing that needed hanging to keep from wrinkling, rather than chance letting the colors bleed onto their other clothes.

She didn't find underwear for either man, and that conjured up images of them standing in the kitchen naked. She couldn't suppress a whimper. Even the sleeveless tshirts that dripped as she lifted them into the washer, made her think of their tattooed flesh. She didn't even want to think about playing with Demon's studded nipple, or she might volunteer for a drunken orgy between the men. It was bad enough their pricks were hardening before her eyes when she took them to the bathrooms and left them. She'd seen men's dicks before, many times when they sat in a corner at the Lady and whacked off from watching her or one of the other dancers, but none of them had matched what she saw hanging... *Stop that, you're just working yourself up for nothing, they're drunk and you haven't had a sex life for years. It's understandable, but downright dumb.*

She added soap and turned the machine to the shortest cycle. Hopefully their clothes would be dry by the time they'd slept the booze off, providing the howling wind and rain didn't knock the power out first.

She walked into the living room and the two men were slumped on the couch, sleeping. So much for worrying about them wanting to have sex in their drunken state, all she could do was grin at the sight of them. Their torsos were lying on the cushions, long legs spread out on the floor, heads almost touching where they'd fallen over. If she had a camera, the scene would be captured for all time. She pulled two flannel sheets from the linen closet and carefully covered each man. They'd ignored the sheets she gave them earlier in favor of bath towels to cover their equipment, but in the positions they landed, nothing was out of sight. She had to leave the room, or sit in the chair, staring at them—she wasn't that much of a masochist.

The electricity blipped for a few minutes, and she almost panicked. When it came back on, she started turning off lights and making certain the house was locked up, before tossing the clean clothes into the dryer and going to bed. Between the two sexy bikers and the storm, tomorrow promised to be interesting.

*****

She woke from an erotic dream where she was, *oh God, this was no dream*, her leg was propped over the shoulder of Demon, and Knight was licking and sucking her breasts. He was devious in the way he manipulated each breast into hard points waiting for his touch. His lips licked and then sucked a small bit of flesh between them, ringing each nipple until she wanted to grab his head and direct those suctioning lips to the hard nubs.

Demon was no less devious in his teasing of her inner thighs and the seam of her body. His thumbs split the lips of her, "Oh, man, look at what I found. Hey, Knight, take a second to look at this, have you ever seen pussy that was this color pink?" His thumbs pushed up on her thick lips and exposed the tiny hood of her clit, with the little muscle peeking from under the cowl. "Fuck, I see you, little bit, I'll get there soon enough."

Jolly couldn't believe he was actually talking to her body, it was crazy, but she loved it, and her clit loved it, showing its appreciation by making her wiggle her hips and whimper in need. She tried to suppress the noises she was making, but that wasn't possible. His tongue was licking closer and closer to her clit with each small cry from her, or it seemed like it to her. Knight finally held her breasts in his hands and pushed them together so the travel time between nipples was miniscule.

160

His fingers circled the wrinkled areolas and his lips gave each a strong suck, repeating over and over again, driving her need. She arched her back when he lifted his head, and cried out when his fingers began pinching the nipples harder, pulling them up and twisting them. It was a sensation that was almost painful, but she loved it, and wanted more. She was panting by the time Knight finally used his tongue to explore every crevice of her mouth and lips.

Jolly felt Demon's tongue finally flicking at her clit and cried out into the mouth that was glued to hers, and his tongue retreated. His lips ended the kiss but didn't leave her skin. Instead he traveled down the ridge of her jawline, trailing to the base of her neck and shoulder. The feeling of his hot breath over the moist trail from his lips made her shiver. When her clit was sucked from its hiding place to be tormented between Demon's teeth, she began to shake. The two long fingers he slid inside her vaginal entrance undid her. She screamed her pleasure through clenched jaws. His fingers continued to push in and out for long minutes afterwards, making her hips twitch from his touch on the over sensitive nerves.

Knight let go of her nubs and her back bowed from the feeling of the blood returning to her nipples, at the same time Demon's fingers worked her G-spot into another body clenching orgasm.

"That's right, ride my fingers. You have the sweetest tasting pussy I've ever eaten, now let's see how much you like my cock." She whimpered, raising her hips to meet his prick as he crawled up to kneel between her spread thighs. Her channel was still clenching from the last orgasm, but he pushed himself slowly inside.

There was no way to describe what he felt while her tunnel was being widened to accommodate his large size. Knight's body was blocking his view of her face as he kept sinking into her tight wet heat.

He didn't know she was digging her nails into his friend's arm, and being mouth fucked with Knight's tongue as she struggled to take his cock. All he felt were tight muscles surrounding his thick prick, and each inch caused her channel to clench, making it almost impossible for him to establish a rhythm until she was wide enough to take him easily. She wasn't a virgin, but he'd bet she was damn close. "Like sticking my cock in a fucking vise, you keep clamping this pussy on me like that and I'm not gonna last much longer. Let up a little."

His hands grabbed the cheeks of her ass, and lifted her up to his prick so he didn't have to bow his back, or have Knight move out of the way. His view was better in this position too. "Ah fuck, man, feed her your prick. With lips like those, I bet it's like fucking this tight pussy."

Knight looked back at him and grinned. He turned back to Jolly and looked into her eyes. He could see she liked the idea from the way she looked down to where his dick was standing erect and licked those sexy lips he couldn't stop kissing. Demon was working her body trying to get deeper inside her, and he wasn't about to stick his own cock in her mouth while her body was moving so jerkily. He shook his head. "Not happening until you get inside, I've seen what happens when you seat that donkey dick of yours. She might end up biting my damn junk off."

Jolly tried to keep silent while her greedy pussy was being stretched to the max. Demon's prick was thicker than she could have imagined, but she found the idea of tasting Knight's impressive cock to be something she almost desperately wanted. He leaned down and started sucking on her nipple again and she felt Demon hit as deep as he could go inside of her. When his prick kissed her cervix, she began to shake. *Holy fuck that hurt, but in a good way*, and she wanted more. When he began to draw out, she pushed her hips up, trying to recapture his marvelous thickness. She no longer cared if they heard her cries.

"Oh yes, more, I want, need more," was screamed without a thought to silence. Demon began a slow sliding rhythm and she did her best to meet him on the downward thrust and kept pumping her hips to her own rhythm. When her hips were lowered to the mattress, she groaned in frustration. "Dammit, stop teasing and fuck me."

Knight leaned further over her and said, "You might want to curb that demand a little, princess, Demon is trying not to tear you up by giving that pussy the pounding you deserve. Yelling at him will just egg him on, and you won't like it if he fucks you raw the first time." He shifted his body on the bed, and tapped her lips with his cock. "Now that he's in, you can put that mouth to good use, no teeth. Open wide and show me what a set of lips like yours around my cock feels like."

He tasted like, she couldn't find anything in her memory to match what his flesh tasted like. There was a hint of soap, but she ignored that as her tongue swirled around the head of his prick, and the small bunch of skin located just under the cleft of the heart shaped head. He was more than a mouthful for sure, and she tried to suck him into her mouth as deeply as she could without gagging. The idea of possibly gagging with his prick in her mouth wasn't exactly romantic. So she took him only until the back of her throat began to strain, then backed off and took him back to the same spot time after time while he held her head and told her that she was, "Fuckin' hot to watch," while she sucked his cock. By the time she felt his shaft begin to pulse, Demon had his hands full of her breasts, as his cock picked up a faster harder rhythm making her groan around the meat in her mouth. Knight pushed deeper into her throat, as the cum shot from his big prick, causing her to either swallow or choke. She swallowed as much as she could and felt him tremble slightly as she continued to suck his dick.

Demon slammed his cock deep and he felt every small grasp of her pink flesh on his cock. His flinger flicked her clit and she went off in a blaze of strong spasms surrounding his prick, milking him as he hosed her with his cum. "Fuck, princess, I'm dying here." He stayed in place long enough for her to ride out the orgasm that had her body strung as tight as it could be.

The three of them laid there for long minutes, before she finally spoke. "That was amazing, just completely amazing."

Demon propped himself up on his arm and grinned down at her. "It only gets better from here." He trailed a finger around her nipples, causing them to harden again, and trailed that finger down around her stomach and to the top of her clit. That finger slid through the slit it found, and gently rubbed back and forth, before sliding through the soaked lips of her cunt and penetrating the entrance to the core of her.

"I like that you like what we did, and I know you're a hot little piece, but you need to understand a few things. Number one, you never refuse this," he curled his fingers inside her and pulled upwards with his words, "to either me or Knight. Number two, you don't fuck anybody but us while we're together unless we say so, and we won't. Consider yourself our property and there shouldn't be a problem. Number three, you got a problem with us, you tell us, you don't go running off to daddy and causing a shit storm over nothing." His fingers continued to saw in and out of her cunt as he spoke.

Knight took up where Demon had become quiet. "Number four, you need to understand the lingo, calling you a bitch or a slut to us, is like some candy ass calling his woman darling or sweetheart. So don't get all pissy if you hear it coming from either of us. Number five, no disrespecting us, especially in front of the members. You got an issue, save it for later, keep that talented tongue of yours behind your teeth. You won't like what happens if you forget it."

Demon increased the speed of his fingers, and could feel her body begin to clamp and release, yeah, she was ready. "We'll give you all of the pleasure one woman can handle as long as the arrangement lasts. I can feel you getting ready to come, go for it, I got you. You're so fuckin' beautiful when you come like this."

She turned her head on the pillow and screamed while the sensations his fingers pulled from deep inside her body took a hold of her. Knight was hugging her upper torso close and she bit him on the shoulder raking her short nails down his forearm, still moving her hips to the rhythm Demon's fingers set.

It took a few minutes for her to come back to reality and see that the men still had hard-ons and were smiling at her with intent. She grinned back at them. "A woman could get used to the two of you and she might get the wrong impression." She sat up and moved her legs into a more comfortable position.

"Before we go for round two here, let me make sure I understand what you're saying. I'm supposed to like being called those names. I can't ever say 'sorry, boys, not tonight, I have a headache'." She was ticking off each "rule" with the fingers of her hand. "I can't call you an asshole, for example, in front of your buddies. I stay monogamous, while you two fuck anything you please. And I can't tell my father anything about us, because he'll probably have you killed for making me unhappy. Is that what I just understood you two saying? Because if it is, I'll take a pass. If all I get from the relationship is great sex, I can get that from any man or men that pride themselves on a job well done."

Jolly climbed off the bed and stood on trembling legs, whose muscles had been stretched in new and wonderful ways. "You don't know me if you think I'm the kind of woman that'll be a fuck buddy that treats you like you're more than casual lovers.

"I have a bit of bad news for you two. You don't get to tell me what to do, how to think, or what I can or can't say. You want respect? You want a mindless fuck doll, not a woman. I don't sleep around because I've seen too many discarded toys walking around with the self-esteem of a whipped puppy." She shook her head at the two men she knew she'd have a hard time forgetting when they left, but she *was not* going to become what they wanted.

"You can't tell me to just respect you, try earning it. You want me to trust your words, but you obviously don't trust me, or you wouldn't have had to tell me not to fuck around. You want, you want. How about what I want? You might be the best sex I've ever had, that's true, but when you consider I've only had one other man, who's to say I couldn't find someone equally good or maybe even better?"

That got a reaction out of both men. If she wasn't feeling so fragile at the moment, she would have laughed. Their eyes narrowed at the mere mention of another man. Maybe, just maybe, they were worth taking the time and risk of creating a relationship. "Thanks for the morning sex, it was a great way to wake me up this morning." She turned away and went to the dresser to get clean clothes for the day, and walked out of the bedroom.

Gladys called as Jolly made a pot of coffee. She wanted to know how much damage the storm had caused, and to tell her, "Georgie finally woke up around five this morning, and started yelling that his head hurt. He almost fell out of bed when I told him to shut it and stop his whining. The nurse pumped his ass full of pain meds and he's sleeping again. They're taking another cat scan today to make sure he's out of danger, and once I hear he'll be okay, I'm coming home. He won't need me, and the Bastards can take it from there."

She told Jolly where the chainsaws were kept, "Although I'm pretty sure we'll have to call someone to use them. Even if we can pick them up, and cut a few small branches or trees, there's no way that either one of us will be able to haul the wood." She also really wanted a clean change of clothing. They chatted a few minutes more, and Jolly promised to be there as soon as she got her shit together for the day.

Rather than follow her inclination of letting the men fend for themselves, she started to mix the batter for baking soda biscuits, and when they were put in the oven to bake, she fried sausage and made white gravy to smother over the biscuits. Two fried eggs on the side of each plate, and breakfast was ready as far as she was concerned. It wasn't fancy, but it would stay with them, and maybe soak up any excess alcohol obviously still messing with their better judgment. She yelled down the hall, "If you're hungry, breakfast is waiting, if not, go without. By the way, your clothes are in the dryer."

CHAPTER SEVENTEEN

Knight woke up first, and saw he'd been sleeping for over an hour after Jolly left the room. He got off the bed and smacked Demon with a pillow, before leaving the room to find his clothes, and that evil little bitch. She had some nerve talking to them like that. They'd offered her things some of the club's bitches would have jumped at the chance to have. The right to call themselves property of Demon and Knight wasn't something to scoff at. It wasn't like they'd ever offered the prestige to any other woman before. She obviously had no idea what she was turning down here.

He found the laundry room and pulled the clothes from the dryer, taking them to the wide leather couch. He sorted his from Demon's and when he was pulling the static socks from the bottom of the pile, he saw a little G-string set of panties, and had to swallow. *Yeah, she was evil alright*. How dare she throw her underwear and tshirts in the same wash with him and Demon's clothing.

Demon came into the room and saw what he was holding, "Fuck, man, what the hell happened between us telling her the good news, and her leaving the room?"

The sight of two heaping plates of breakfast food sitting on the counter that had long gone cold made them smile. Maybe it was her way of apologizing for being such a bitch about their offer. They nuked the food and ate every bite. They finished the coffee, but she still hadn't shown her skinny little ass. They went looking through every room and not finding her, they went outside to check on things. Her mustang was missing from the barn. Since they weren't going anywhere until they cleared the path between the road and their bikes, they grabbed a chainsaw and a plastic jug filled with a gallon of gasoline, before going to find where the bikes were trapped.

They borrowed the electric cart Gladys used around the campground to carry themselves and the equipment back to the road and down the hundred feet or so to the path where their bikes sat. There were several branches that had fallen in the storm and some of them required the men cut them and remove them from the path, before they could move forward. It was hotter than hell by the time they'd stripped the branches off the huge old tree, and the men were worn out from using muscles they'd forgotten they had.

"I don't know about you, but my throat's dryer than a popcorn fart, and I need something to drink before we tackle the rest of this mess." Knight sat the chainsaw on the ground near the huge tree trunk. "That breakfast princess made for us is gone by now, I need food. This is work, and it feels good to be out here working, but damn, man, I'm going to have to hit the weight room more often."

Demon sat on the four foot long, twelve inch thick branch he'd been attempting to move from the spot it had embedded into the dirt. "Yeah, my arms feel numb like they're gonna fall off. I haven't had a workout like this in forever. Aside from the obvious fact that we won't have this thing cut up and out of the way before it gets dark, I need to hydrate and inhale some calories too. Let's pack it up and come back in a couple of hours, do some damage, and then we can get the bikes out sometime in the morning. If we're lucky maybe princess will cook something again."

Knight looked at him and Demon shrugged, "I've been thinking about what she said. She's right, we don't *know* her, we *want* her, big fuckin' difference to some women."

Jolly wasn't at the house when they got back. She still wasn't back when they finished for the night either. The house was dark inside, and nothing had been touched as far as they could tell. Concern overrode irritation. Where the hell was she?

Knight checked his phone, and found his battery was drained so dry the only thing the damn thing would do was briefly light up to tell him 'Battery is Low'. Demon's phone had met his temper yesterday when he had his hands on Fuller. The little fucker tried to kick him in the nuts to make him let go. Demon had moved out of his range, and got kicked in the pocket with his expensive phone inside. The damn fragile thing was done for. He looked at the worthless piece of plastic and threw it at the stone fireplace. He didn't bother to watch it shatter.

They were stomping around trying to decide what to do. Knight had his hand on the door heading for the barn where he figured he could hotwire the truck, when they heard a phone ringing in the office. Demon rushed inside the small room and snatched up the receiver, "Yeah?"

Knight saw his friend slump onto the leather office chair and hang his head for a minute while he listened to whoever was on the other end of the line. "Yes, we're starving, and Gladys is out of beer. Yeah, good, be careful." He gently hung the plastic back in its cradle and got to his feet. He walked through the kitchen and out the back door. Knight followed him, wondering what was going on. Demon stopped at the woodpile where there were logs in various sizes stacked on one side, and a small shed that came close to losing its door to the giant redhead. He sat a log up on the old stump and whacked it with the splitting maul, before beginning to talk.

"She's fine, Gladys is staying another night with Georgie, and Jolly wasn't sure if we would be here or not, so she wanted to know if we wanted her to bring home pizza." That piece of wood fell aside and he continued to take his aggression out on the wood, "If I don't get some of this out of my system, I will bust her ass the minute she walks in the door. The only thing that will accomplish is her having a beautiful red ass, and I'll end up fucking her until she's ready to admit she belongs to you and me."

Knight sat down hard when Demon said that Jolly was fine. "When I saw her the first time, I could tell she'd been running from something, and it wasn't something she wasn't used to doing either. She was living on nerves, and her hair was chopped, you wouldn't recognize her from the bloody mess she was that morning. I'd even say she's gained a few pounds since then. The only thing that's the same about her is those big old green eyes and the way my dick gets hard looking at her. It was damn confusing. Have you noticed how small her wrists are? They were just skin covering bones last time I saw her. She was a mouthy bitch, and protective, but she kicked that fucker Dorsey with her bare feet, and probably broke a few toes, but didn't even flinch. It was fuckin' hot to see her standing there like a wacked out zombie slut."

He shook his head, "There wasn't one damn thing about her that should've made my dick stir to life, but it did."

Demon continued to take his irrational anger out on the wooden victims of the splitting maul. *It's not just sex you dumb bastard, she has that special something, just like Knight said.* That didn't mean he was going to promise the woman anything permanent. As long as it lasted, she'd have their protection, and enjoy as much sex as she could handle. When it ran its course, no harm no foul, everyone parted company and moved on with their lives.

That crack she'd made about not sleeping around to avoid becoming a fuck toy, easily discarded, was bullshit. He'd never tried to make a woman fall in love with him, he'd always been up front and enjoyed the exchange of sexual gratification. Why couldn't Jolly understand that? If she wanted them to keep their dicks in their pants all she had to do was say so. Women were so damn complicated, it pissed him off. He didn't like worrying about her today, she should have left a fucking note or something, and he planned to explain that to her, just not until he was calmer.

He and Knight had decided to try having an old lady a chance for a while. It wouldn't be like marriage for crissakes, and not like they planned to have kids with her or anything.

Kids changed everything. He wouldn't take the chance that his kid would be abandoned by him, that was for damn certain. Knight's father, the mean old bastard that he was, at least he'd treated Demon like his own kid. When one of the boys got in trouble, both of them paid the price. For all his meanness and old school shit, the man had been the only constant adult male in Demon's life. He'd been happy when his mother shacked up with the old man.

He heard the sound of the Mustang drive up, but ignored it. The pile of wood still hadn't managed to calm his temper enough. He'd have blisters, but they'd be a reminder of how much trouble women caused. He worked steadily through the first stack and moved onto the second wearing his arms out. It was getting too dark for him to see what he was doing, and his body was totally wrecked, just as badly as his mind. His plan to take a hot shower and scarf something down his gullet was all he focused on as he headed to the house.

He walked into the kitchen, snagged a slice of cold pizza out of the cardboard box on the counter, and then going through the room, entering the hallway bathroom. The last bite was in his mouth before he opened the door, and almost choked at the sight of Jolly entering the shower enclosure.

She made a squeaking noise and quickly shut herself behind the sliding glass, but all that did was increase the sudden awareness that Demon was three feet away, and Knight had just worked her over with his words and big body.

She'd gotten home and carried the two large pizza boxes inside first, and after setting them on the counter, went back to the car to grab the beer and two bags of clothes she'd purchased for herself. Knight was waiting at the door, shirtless, and sober faced. He took the beer, and she kept going through the house to drop her bags into her bedroom.

She hadn't made it out of the room before Knight had her flat on her back on the bed. He'd had her bent over with her jeans around her ankles and his fingers in her snatch before she even considered protesting. "You've been a bad princess, leaving us with no idea where you were going or when you'd be back. Our woman should know better than that shit, and by the time we're done tonight, she will."

Jolly felt a thrill at his macho bullshit attitude. Having him manhandle her like he did outraged her and sent shivers to that inner slut that'd been reminding her of being filled with Demon's cock every time she moved her legs today. While she shopped for new underwear, and new jeans, she'd seen a pair of four inch heels that appealed to that slut in a very dirty way. It'd been a couple of years since she'd indulged in sexy shoes, and it'd been hard to resist those shoes today. Her panties were soaked by the time she'd gotten back to the campground.

She expected Knight to slam his cock inside her once he found out she was wet and ready before he'd even touched her, but he surprised her by finger fucking her needy flesh first. Her token protest of, "I'm not your woman," had gotten her a sharp slap on the ass. All that did was amp up her excitement.

"Now see? You should have kept your mouth shut and not said that to me, because now I'm going to have to show you that you are my woman, and when Demon works the worry for you out of his system, he'll show you the error of your thoughts too." He added a third finger to the first two and she thrilled at the feeling of fullness.

"Are you ready to have your first lesson in being my woman?" Her whimper told him all he needed to know, that and the way her ass pushed back on his thigh as his fingers stroked through her tender flesh. He set his cock at the tight entrance ring of muscle guarding her channel. "Push back on this, princess, let's see if you enjoy being fucked from behind as much as you enjoyed it flat on your back. Damn, woman, I thought my fingers widened you more than this." His prick was being held tight within her heat, and he slowly penetrated her soft flesh, but the urge to fuck her raw was riding him, so he began short jabs and slaps on her ass cheeks.

"You will be ours, you will be respectful, and you will like it our way." He could finally slide his full length inside. He took advantage of the wet slide to double the speed and strength of his thrusts. From her squeals and the way she was panting for breaths, he knew she liked it so he slammed home even harder.

Jolly couldn't argue with him right this minute, she'd worry about his demands later. Right now, she felt her body tightening up, building into the orgasm she'd been craving all day. Those sharp stings on her ass only made her want to spread her legs wider and take him even deeper, but her jeans were around her ankles and he was, holy fuck, she felt his wet thumb press on her butthole distracting her from that needed orgasm for a moment. "What do you think, oh god, fuck me, yeah, just like that."

The thumb was momentarily forgotten while he reached down under her bent hips and pinched her clit. She hurt her own ears from the pitch of her scream as her body electrified, the heat washed over her face and neck and traveled down her body. That thumb slid all the way into her asshole and she felt every time he flexed his thick digit. It only added to her pleasure. She felt the heat of his cum being pumped deep inside and as her tunnel clamped and released his prick, she could feel the pulse of his release. Knowing she was responsible for the jerking way he was now moving inside her body increased her pleasure, and she broke into a million pieces. Nothing had ever come close to the way these men made her feel,

He pulled his thumb from her ass, and stepped back so his prick had room to exit its warm cocoon. He used both hands to massage the cheeks of her ass, and gave them a squeeze. "One of these days, you're going to have Demon in your cunt and me in this sweet ass of yours, and you're going to love it."

Thirty minutes later, they'd eaten one of the pizzas and she handed her car keys over to him when he asked to borrow her car. "Just be careful with my baby. Or I'll be forced to learn to drive a bike and take your hog in trade." The look he'd given her was priceless.

The steady thunking sound of Demon's labors had a cadence about the rhythm, and she grinned as she made her way to the bedroom for fresh sleepwear and into the bathroom. "I don't know but I get told, biker's cocks are made of gold." The silly lyrics made her giggle and laugh. She stripped out of her clothing, and stepped into the shower enclosure just as the door opened, and Demon stepped in the open doorway. She quickly pulled the glass slider closed and stood under the hot spray of water.

Demon knew by the time he was halfway through that pile of wood that he was sinking. He denied it to himself until the blood blisters on his hands broke open and began to seep. He didn't believe in romantic kissy faced love, but he couldn't deny the feeling of abandonment when they'd came back to the campground and found the house empty. The pep talk he'd given himself while splitting that mountain of wood had only clarified his emotional situation.

When he saw Jolly's naked flank stepping into the shower and that silhouette of her body behind the opaque glass, his cock stirred to life. The damned thing didn't care the rest of his body was too fucking tired to function. His prick was the only muscle he hadn't abused today. He didn't give into the lure of joining her in the small space. Instead, he went down the hall and let himself into the other bathroom, stripping before adjusting the temperature, and stepping under the water. His dick was just going to have to wait until he was ready to make his final decision.

CHAPTER EIGHTEEN

Knight saw crazy Charlie, Joker, and Pressley sitting in the corner drinking and talking. Joker and Pressley got up and headed toward the back door. Charlie sat by himself, staring at his longneck, and the packet of sugar next to it. Knight got a beer from Tiny and joined the greybeard. He'd become fond of the old guy, but something wasn't quite right about him this evening.

"Hey, brother, what's up? It's so fucking quiet in the club tonight, I wondered if I walked into the right place."

Charlie shook his head, "We got turned back by that damn storm last night. We were about half way up, and the wind started howling and rain started pouring, I can pretty much guarantee the sniper ain't dedicated enough to hang around in those trees when the lightning was zapping everything it could touch. Tonight we're supposed to get another storm. They're already saying tornados, so we came back until tomorrow if the rain lets up."

Knight nodded his head, the wind had already started blowing again before he'd parked the car in front of the building, so he wasn't surprised at Charlie's news. It looked like most of the members were staying close to home tonight, and he didn't blame them a bit. If he hadn't needed a change of clothes and time to think, he'd still be at the campground with Jolly and Demon. The clothes were just steps away, but the thinking, that hung over his chest like a big fucking rock.

"I needed to do some thinking and deciding on a few things, and damned if I'm any closer to either one than when I started."

Charlie nodded in agreement. "Hell yes, I played the nice guy, and all I am is miserable. You know I planned to make Selma my old lady and set up housekeeping, right? Well, she started talkin' bout buying me a suit, and cutting my beard off. She wants to be elected to that judge's position at the County Family Court, and I was all for it, until she started trying to change me. She said I look too much like a disreputable biker with the beard and tats. I told her that's 'cause I am a disreputable biker, and don't plan to change. Damn, man, I ain't wore a suit since I graduated from the eighth grade at St Mary's. Well then, and my dress blues."

For obvious reasons, Knight had to agree with Charlie, if a woman needed to change him, he wouldn't take too kindly to that either. "That sucks, man, sorry to hear that. I know you were getting seriously involved with the woman. That's nuts, she knew what you were before you two started seeing each other." Charlie nodded his head in agreement and upended the bottle. "So what are you going to do about the situation?"

"Well I ain't planning anything now. I took the high road and told her it was better for her if I just let her fly solo. I cut her loose. All my fault and we can be friends, and shit like that. I got no reason to cuss her. I knew she was smarter than me to begin with. I could deal with buying the woman little gifts and bringing her a box of chocolates every once in a while. Hell, you know how much women like them little things. They gotta think they're the most important thing in a man's life. Maybe if I was thirty years younger and not so set in my ways, I might compromise a little more. Hell, who am I kidding, I ain't gonna change. I was even wilder then than I am nowadays. She cried, and I left." He stood and hurled the empty bottle in the trashcan. "Ain't nothing good coming out on the short end of the stick like this, but she can be happy with her little black robe and gavel, making her dream come true, and I'll be ridin' the roads like I always do." He walked to the bar and snagged a couple more longnecks placing one in front of Knight who sat contemplating the old man's words of wisdom.

He didn't know what was eating at the younger man, but with that kind of blank look, it had to be woman troubles. "You know, seems like there's something in the air around here lately. Me and Selma, Big Dog and Future, Beadle deserves his misery, so I got no sympathy for him. George, well he's a hard case, and if he don't get his head outta his ass, he's gonna lose Gladys too.

"Tiny is home with his ol' lady tonight, he left here like his tail was on fire. Said he wasn't taking any chances that Lila would catch whatever's going around. You see the way Tarzan and Seth dote on Harlow. Pressley was tellin' us that he was thinking about making Tinkerbelle into a house mouse. Tiny's woman is a smart one, she saves her bitchin' for when he's home, never seen her say shit to him here in front of the brothers, and that was when she had cause.

"So, what has your dick in a knot tonight?" While he waited for Knight to get around to talking, he watched Teach's technique as the man buried his face between Pinky's thighs. "Ain't no way Pinky'll come that way. He's licking, but if he don't pay attention to that clit of hers, she ain't gonna get her goodies. Pinky likes her clit sucked on and her tits are real sensitive too. If the man ever watched what she does to get herself off while he was plowing her pussy, he'd know she needs that little bit of extra incentive. Dumb fucker thinks a few licks and pokes are enough for a woman. Any man that thinks him tellin' a woman what she wants is how it goes, hell that's just dirt dumb.

"We can only hope one day he's gonna figure that out. There ain't nothin' stronger than a woman. You tell me one thing you think's stronger," he demanded from Knight who had no idea what the old man wanted him to ask. Women were strong, hell they had to be, but to say they were stronger than a man, was just wrong.

"I know they have strength, Charlie, no disrespect, but not many women can match the strength of a man, it's not their fault, it's just the way they're built."

Charlie laughed in his face. "I was with a couple of them when they birthed babies. You ain't seen strength till you see a woman push out a baby, then laugh and cry about it afterwards. Put a woman in a fuckin' cave with a dirt floor and she'll make that cave a goddamned cozy nest. Before he knows it, her man gets used to the luxuries and does his best to keep her happy. Cave or mansion. It don't matter to most women as long as her man stays true and makes her feel like she's important and not just for fuckin'. You ain't ever seen anything more loyal or deadly than a woman defending what's hers.

"I knew a woman that stood over her man, who was bleeding to death by the way, and had two little kids hanging on her skirts. She stood over them with an old double barrel, she was ready to kill ol' Fred the Chinaman. Course that was back in the biker wars, and there wasn't any place for her to take cover with them. The Ghouls had burned the house down. We came up on them before she had to shoot. Not that it would've been a shame if she'd done the world a favor.

"All I'm saying is that any man who thinks a woman's weak, deserves it when she hands him his nuts and walks out. That's why I decided on Selma. She's everything I admire in a woman. Strong, and you might not know it to look at her now, but she was always a beauty. You shoulda seen her go after Joker when he got to making fun of me thinking about domestic shit. To you and me it was just him trying to bust my balls. To her? She was ready to gut his ass."

Charlie was laughing in remembrance of the way Selma had gotten that haughty look on her face and narrowed her eyes at Joker. She'd actually tried to stand in front of him while she verbally started cutting his old friend down to size. It'd taken a few long kisses and, hahaha, yeah a good fuck, before she calmed down enough to listen to him tell her about men busting each other's chops. That had put the bracelet on his ankle as far as he was concerned.

A woman that was smarter than he would ever hope to be, defending him like she'd done, made him near to bursting with pride to be the man she took home with her.

"Might as well face the facts, if all you got in common, or can find to admire a woman for is her ability to fuck or suck, then you ain't gonna invest the time to get to know her. You find a woman that you can talk to, and I don't mean sex talk or get me a beer talk. She might teach you what you don't know."

Charlie got up. "I got things to look into tonight." He left Knight sitting there feeling like he'd been schooled by the old man.

*****

Demon was warming pizza in the microwave when Jolly decided to gather her courage and join him on the porch. She noticed he was moving a little slowly, and he held a bottle of unopened beer between his hands, rolling it back and forth. The microwave dinged, so she pulled his food out and grabbed herself a coke, before finally sitting down and listening to the sounds of nature at night.

"It looks like Gladys will have plenty of firewood when the nights start getting colder. That was really nice of you." He nodded while he chewed. She tried a different track of conversation. "I loaned Knight my car. He said he needed to go to the club and check on a few things, and grab you both some clean clothes. I was planning to hold his hog hostage, but when I looked outside for it, I didn't see either bike. How'd you guys come to be in the vicinity when the storm hit?"

185

He wiped his fingers on his pant leg, and cracked the top of the beer open, after taking a long pull from the bottle, he pointed to the back of the property. "There's a spot next to this place that nobody claims, and it's a good place to study a problem. Knight and I had some problem solving to do, so we stopped there. The storm came up, and this huge damn tree fell right behind the bikes. There we were, no place to hide and dodging lightning bolts. We spent all day today clearing the path to the bikes, but that huge tree needs a few more men to move the trunk, providing we can get the thing chopped into pieces manageable enough to move."

He became quiet, and picked up another slice of pizza, then tossed it back onto the plate. "When you weren't here at two o'clock when we took a break, it wasn't a big deal. When we came back at seven, and you were still gone, it bothered us. We had no transportation, and no cell phones 'cause mine's broken, and Knight's was out of juice. If the office phone hadn't rung, we would have really been upset. I was getting ready to hotwire that old truck in the barn when you called all humming and chirpy as a bird.

"Let's just say that pile of wood saved your ass from my hand busting it. I don't worry about people. I figure they can take care of themselves." He picked up the pizza again, and took a large bite.

Jolly couldn't believe they were actually having a conversation that didn't involve him telling her what she was going to do. To be honest, he was kind of hinting at his feelings on the subject of her absence. On the bright side, at least he wasn't demanding she do his bidding either. Yet, that three letter word was small, but always hanging in the air when he talked.

"I didn't mean to worry either of you. I wanted to see Gladys and while I was in town, I did some exploring. I found a couple of small places that had some clothes I needed, so I took my time. It didn't occur to me you'd still be here, until I started thinking about supper. That's why I called to see if you were still here so I'd bring home plenty to eat. I'm not in the habit of feeding a man, let alone two huge men. You have to admit, you two aren't the average six foot tall hundred-eighty pound guys." It was her turn to take a drink from her coke stalling for time.

"I spent most of today thinking about what you and Knight told me, and once I got over being mad and hurt, I tried to look at it from your point of view. I still can't turn myself into a fuck toy for the two of you, tempting as it may be, I have to live with myself. I loved what we did, there's no use in denying that, and great sex is a big plus on my list of what I need in a relationship.

"You see, I'm not the kind of woman that goes into a relationship looking for the end. If and when I agree to take that step, I'll be looking forward to the future, happy to be heading toward a home and kids type of arrangement." He kept chewing and nodding his head, but she didn't hold out a lot of hope he understood what she was saying. "Rationally I know you guys are sincere, and to you, what you've offered is a compliment. My mother thought she was getting more than William was offering. She hung her heart out for him to stomp on, and she never let herself care for another man. She wasn't a masochist, but she cut herself off from the possibility of being hurt again by simply refusing to allow another man to change her mind. I refuse to let myself get into a position that ruins my self-esteem and life. I'm a person, and I don't want or need to have someone tell me what I can or can't do."

He was staring at her blank faced, but at least he didn't appear mad. "If there's love in a relationship, trusting in that person should be enough until they screw it up. My opinion should matter, I have a brain, and I know how to use it most of the time."

He just kept staring at her and it was making her more nervous. "Look, you can talk you know, I've been blabbering all this time, and haven't heard a word come out of your mouth." It took him a few minutes, but she was happy she'd waited once he began to talk.

"Nail Faultersak, I'm thirty-two years old. I have most of my teeth. I served two tours in the Middle East, and I speak four languages fluently enough to ask where the bar and bathrooms are." He finished his beer, and continued his list. "I was raised by my mother and Knight's father. My old man took off sometime between the diapers and the rent coming due, so my mother worked her ass off to keep us fed and a roof over our heads. I spent a lot of time hanging at Knight's house. His dad is one mean sonofabitch, but I love the old fart.

"While Knight and I were overseas, the old man checked on my mother for me, and when we got back, they were living together. I took the money I saved while I was deployed, and bought into a tool company that manufactures maintenance equipment for several different areas of manufacturing. Knight bought into the same company, and we don't have to do a thing there but collect our checks. So we started buying houses at auction, and without being falsely modest, we made a shit ton of money rehabbing and selling them. We got the club in on that gig, and when the market crashed on housing, and people were losing their houses right and left, we snapped a bunch up. Rentals are a main source of income for the club now."

Demon wondered what she thought about him telling her his life story, well as much as he could share with her for now. He stood, and winced every step of the way to the fridge to nab another beer.

Jolly winced from watching him, thinking he was a typical macho asshole. They jump right into doing some heavy work without stretching or working up to the challenge. She knew she could help alleviate the pain he was feeling right now, and the pain he'd deal with tomorrow wouldn't be as intense as it would be if she left him to suffer. She sighed, it wouldn't be a hardship to work over those thick muscles covering his body, in fact, she could feel that slut inside of her grinning in anticipation.

She stopped him from heading back to the porch. "I'll tell you what, big guy, since I can't stand to watch you groan and grunt with every step, why don't you wait a minute and I'll grab a sheet to cover the carpet." She hurried into the hallway and came back with a large flannel sheet, and a bottle of body oil she'd picked up today, thinking about rubbing out her legs after a long day of working in the campground as Gladys had warned her.

She spread the sheet on the carpet, and, "Okay, you'll need to buck down, so I can work on those tree trunks you call legs." He nodded and made his way over to where she'd set up shop. "You don't have to worry that I'll hurt you. I have a certification in Massage Therapy, and two years of college, where I planned to get a degree in Nursing."

CHAPTER NINETEEN

Demon did his best not to groan while getting to his knees, and had to hold onto the couch cushions while he lowered his naked body to the floor. "You can't hurt me, princess, bigger men than you have tried." The groan that escaped him when he finally settled on his stomach, with his arms at his sides, embarrassed him, but right now, he couldn't care less. He still couldn't resist teasing her a little. "I think it's only fair that if I have to be naked, you should at least ditch those ugly shorts. Don't you have a bikini or something?"

She knelt next to his side and poured a generous stream of oil down his spine. "Yes I bought a bikini, but I've gained so much weight in the last two weeks I can't wear it. Thing is, you don't seem to understand something here. I offered to give you a massage to ease your pain, not as foreplay. Giving a man a massage doesn't mean I plan to play the whore. You can get other benefits from what I do. So why don't you shut it and let me do what I can to help these muscles you abused today?"

She spread oil over his shoulders and the small of his back, giving them a light rub, before crawling down to his feet. Oiling up her hands she started working from his toes up into his calves.

He startled her with his demand, "Tell me about you. Why were you on the run, and what's the deal about just finding out William Kelly is your father? It'll help take my mind off the pain." He wanted her story, and he told her the truth, listening to her sexy voice talking did help take his mind off his body aches and pains.

It kind of bugged her that Demon and Knight kept calling her princess. She wondered why they'd picked a name like that to tag her with, but his request for information about her life seemed harmless enough. There was no reason for her to hide anymore. William had made sure she understood that Porter and James wouldn't be harming anyone again.

"Well, my name was always a mystery, it's not like people really name their kids Jolly. Other emotions make good names, like Cherish, but now that I think about it, that's not a great name either. Hope, that's a good name. Anyway, it seems William used to call my mother Jolly when they had their fling, because she was always happy and smiling."

She dug her fingers into the tight muscle of his thigh, finding the knots and holding pressure on the knot until it released its tightness, and she moved on to the next one. "Since this is going to take a while, I'll give you the long boring version of my story. By the time I'm done, you'll probably be asleep."

She started her tale at the tender age of six, and by the time she'd gotten to the reason for her stint as a pole dancer, he was asking questions, in between moaning and groaning. Her hands seemed to love the feel of his glutes, they were more than a handful of solid muscle, and she thoroughly worked on those delectable rounds, before working her way up his back and shoulders. Her hands made long slow strokes over his smooth back. The oil made the tattoos on his skin almost come alive with her manipulation of the flesh and muscle beneath them.

"So you've been running for over two years with little or no money, and no one to help you? How in the hell did you survive?"

"Time to roll over, big guy, I can get to the front of your thighs easier and your chest has muscles that need to be stretched too." She patted his ass, and sat back from his side so he could move. Shaking out the cramping in her fingers while he warned her.

"You gave me a chubby, so don't freak out when I roll over and you get to see what you caused, princess."

She was impressed with his 'chubby' as he called it, but no way that thing could be called merely chubby. She looked at his prick, and looked back at his face to talk. If she didn't look at his face she might give into temptation and rub the tension out of *that* muscle, and after her lecture about therapy massages, that wouldn't do at all. It would be too hard to convince him that she hadn't wanted to get him excited, all she wanted was to take his pain away. She tossed a hand towel over his hips. His prick tented the terry cloth, but at least she was fighting the good fight. *Taking the high road, and it sucked.*

Jolly shook her head, "If that's what you call a chubby, then you haven't been watching as much porn as you bikers are reputed to watch. Don't you guys sit around whacking off and watching women lick each other while you have a woman giving you oral sex? Or is my education lacking in biker lore?"

She began again at his toes, working her way up his thick calves and thighs. "The pervs used to jack off in the dark corners at the Lady, we all saw them. I tried not to look, but sometimes it's like a train wreck. You know?"

Her descriptions weren't much of a surprise to him, but if she was a stripper, "How did you stay almost innocent with a job like that? I know it sounds like I'm judging, but truth is, I've been in strip clubs, and never had a stripper turn down cold hard cash."

She dug her thumbs into his chest muscle and didn't let up until he grunted. "Not every stripper is a whore or prostitute, for your information, it wasn't a job requirement to fuck the patrons. Some of the girls did, I wasn't one of them. I told you, being a discarded fuck toy was never high on my list of things I wanted to do with my life. I danced, I stripped, and I collected my money, then I went home, alone, in that order." She sat back on her knees, and stood.

Demon knew he'd fucked up, but he had to know. Some jealous little bug crawled up his ass, and he had to hear it from her. He reached a hand up, and she thought he wanted help getting off the floor, so she reached down to grasp his hand and found herself on his wide chest.

"I wasn't implying a damn thing. Do you think I couldn't tell that you weren't a whore? Even if Knight hadn't told me about your first meeting, and even after talking to you, the little bits of conversation we've had, there was no signs of you ever being a whore, so stop thinking like that. If nothing else told me what you are, the difficulty in sticking my cock inside your little pussy would be more than enough for any man to know you had very little experience. The only thing indicating your non-virginal status was that I didn't feel a hymen when I finally got inside of you." He stroked her back and held her to his chest with the other arm.

"As for this shit about becoming a fuck toy, you've seen my body, what is the first thing a woman thinks of when she sees me with my clothes on? I'll tell you, because I get told all the time, they want to fuck me. They want to see me naked. Hell, one woman wanted me to let her lick chocolate off my chest while she fucked me, and her old man wanted to take pictures of us like that.

"When women see me naked, they either back off fast, or look at my prick like it's a fucking challenge. They don't give a shit about me, my packaging is attractive to them. Remember you telling us that we don't know you? Try being a horn dog like me and Knight. After a while, fucking is just a bodily function, it doesn't matter if you know the snatch or not. Hell, it don't matter to her what my name is, she's there and eager to have my dick. Afterwards, she goes to her friends and brags that she fucked a guy with a big cock, and I move on until the urge and opportunity hits me again.

"I saw you, and something twisted in my guts, Knight said you have that special something for him too. We had some things to iron out between us before the storm came up, and once we took care of that, the next subject was you. We both want you, I think you figured that out already. We weren't exactly smooth when we offered to make you our old lady. The truth is, we already let one woman like you that had a special appeal for us slip right by. We didn't want that to happen again. Our offer wasn't worded like it should have been, and we sounded like a couple of caveman assholes to you. We rushed it, and I'm sorry, but you need to understand we don't want you to slip past us. Women want love and hearts and flowers and shit like that, but until we can call it love, would you settle for commitment and great sex while we get to know each other better?"

All the while he was talking, his hands had been rubbing her skin. Jolly realized her shorts were down around her knees, and her t-shirt was pulled up in the back almost to her neck. While she thought about his explanation for their offer to make her an old lady, his fingers were pulling her thighs apart, and the shorts slipped off one ankle and he pulled it over his hips. Her clit was mashed against his thick cock, and his hands held the cheeks of her ass as he slid her up and down his length slowly. The glide was easy because she was soaking both of them with her body's juices.

"If you don't want this, say something now. I want inside you more than I want to breathe." His hands clutched her hips continuing the sensual massage of their bodies.

Jolly had to agree with him, she wanted to feel that thick prick deep inside, stretching her vaginal tunnel and kissing her cervix causing that small shock of biting pleasure. "Demon."

He interrupted her. "My name's Nail. I want to hear my name coming from your lips when we're together like this."

Why'd he have to say things like that? Every word he said made sense and gave her hope, because in spite of the short time she'd known him and that arrogant ass Knight, she knew she'd consent to doing whatever she could to make their arrangement work without totally debasing herself and becoming a mindless fuck toy. If she didn't at least try, she knew she'd always wonder what if. She was stronger than her mother, she would live her life to the fullest, with or without the two men. It might kill something inside her if they couldn't love her like she deserved, but she would survive.

She raised her head, and waited for his eyes to open and meet her own. "Make love to me, Nail." She gripped his wide shoulders and pulled herself up to meet his lips with her own, licking the seam. "I love the feeling of your skin against mine." She kissed his jawline. "I love the way you taste on my tongue."

The feeling of his thick cock entering her was amazing. There was no hurry or force, her body absorbed him inside, and she felt the big body beneath her shake. His hands gripped harder on her hips and she braced herself up and back to bring him deeper. Her breath hissed out between her teeth, even as his thickness slid further in, she felt the burn of her channel widening to accommodate his cock. She raised herself up halfway to her knees and slowly lowered herself back over him. On her next down stroke she swiveled her hips to one side slightly and then the other. His hands took possession of her breasts and nipples.

The scrape of rough thumbs rubbing over the tops of her nipples made her gasp and him moan.

"Oh fuck, Jolly, you're driving me crazy, woman. That's right, baby, take all of me you want, just don't fuckin' stop moving, don't stop." He propped himself on his elbows and leaned up to take a hard nipple into his mouth and sucked it strongly mashing it on the roof of his mouth with his tongue. He allowed that breast to bounce back and latched onto the other one. He was moaning and she could feel the vibration travel through her breast. Knowing she was bringing this giant man such pleasure made her body gush even more of its juices and she pushed back harder trying to take the entire length and breadth of his prick.

She sat back onto his hips and sealed their bodies. There was no choice, her body demanded she grind down hard while he was as deep as he could go. The pleasure hit her and she jerked her hips screaming his name and digging her short nails into his wide chest.

Demon had momentarily stopped all movement of his own while he watched her head fling back and the scream come out of her wide mouth. *Fuckin' beautiful.* The little scratches on his chest made him smile. He was entranced by the sight and feel of her pleasure, unaware he was still rubbing her ass cheeks and verbally praising the beautiful woman with the tightest pussy in the world. "You're squeezing me so fuckin' tight I can't move. I can feel the way your pussy is grabbing me, fuckin' awesome."

Jolly kept moving, grinding harder, prolonging her orgasm, and the next one hit her as she began to catch her breath. She let it take her over the edge, as his prick filled her with his milky cum.

She fell on top of his chest and began to laugh, still feeling her vaginal muscles twitch on his deflating prick. He winced each time it happened, and she found it funny that he jerked when her flesh hugged him on his way out.

"Sure, laugh at the crippled guy." He held her on top of him. There was plenty to say, but right now, it felt like the perfect time to just enjoy the quiet together. The wind howled and rain lashed at the metal roof as they walked down the hall, and ended the night cuddled close in her bed.

CHAPTER TWENTY

Gladys called for a ride early in the morning, so Knight drove to the hospital and picked her up. The suburbs looked like a battleground with downed trees and smashed cars. Prindale had been lucky, the town to the west was almost completely destroyed by a tornado that hit during the first wave of storms. More storms were predicted in the next few days, and Knight wanted to get the chopper out of the woods before they hit.

The backseat was loaded with clean clothes for him and Demon. His brain hadn't let him sleep until he examined what Crazy Charlie had told him. His ego finally understood what the old bastard had been saying. The morning call to his birth mother helped him get things straight in his mind. She hadn't left him voluntarily, but she couldn't handle his father's demands. Looking back, he could understand what she told him. His father refused to allow him to leave with her, and she was afraid of what he would do if she tried to take him. "You worshipped him, Lucas, but as much as you loved him, I began to hate the sight of him. If I went to the store for diapers and milk, he swore I was screwing the bag boy. When I went to the doctor, he had to be in the exam room because no one touched his property, even a female doctor. Every time he left for weeks at a time, God help me, I prayed he wouldn't come back home. I loved him, thought the stars hung from his hands, and to be blunt, the makeup sex was fantastic.

"I swear, Lucas, I never stopped caring about you, and it took me years to stop caring about your father. I couldn't take his brand of love anymore. I was done the day I found out I lost a baby because he had been having sex with a woman infected with an STD and then he infected me. I decided to leave when he just shrugged his shoulders and told me to get over it and fix his dinner, he was hungry." He heard her crying as she talked to him for the first time about the breakup.

"I had us packed and the bags in my sister's car when he came home early. He pulled you out of the car seat and told me to get the hell out of his sight. From that day on, until you were twelve years old, the only way he would allow me to see you was for me to come to his house. I had to give him a blowjob while he called me filthy names and did his best to make me sorry I left in the first place. He did other things to me, things I won't talk about, because he knew how much I loved you. The day I stopped coming over to see you," he could hear her blow her nose and take a few deep breaths trying to clear her throat, "I'd called and he told me I could come on Friday night after I got off work. I got there, but you weren't there. He'd done that to me a couple of times before, and I got upset because I'd worked a full day, then drove fifty miles to see my son. I knew he'd done it on purpose again. I threatened to take him to court. I should have just kept my mouth shut and left, but he laughed, so I told him I'd find a good lawyer and if I had to, I'd sleep with the man to get him to represent me in court. Bill went apeshit on me. He dragged me into the trailer and spent the weekend knocking the teeth out of my mouth. I can't tell you all he did to me that weekend, but I never went back, and he wouldn't let me talk to you on the phone.

"I was so happy to hear your voice when I tried one more time on your eighteenth birthday to ask you to meet me, but, well, you know how that turned out.

"You have no idea how happy I am you finally called me. I've been afraid my prayers would never be answered. I figured I had to pay for whatever I'd done for even longer, but now you've called, and asked for the reasons I left. So now you know, it had nothing to do with my love for you, Lucas."

His own eyes were swimming by the time she got his promise to visit her in a week or two. He gave her his phone number, and hated it each time she thanked him for taking the time to call her. Especially since the last time she called he hadn't been nice about it. He didn't remember everything he'd said that day, but from the way the woman cried, he bet she remembered every word of that short conversation. He had asked his mother what she wanted from him and why she bothered to call him after all that time, wasn't exactly what a brokenhearted mother wanted to hear from her boy. He was drunk from celebrating his birthday, but he was certain he'd told her to fuck off and not bother him again.

All of this was too much for him to absorb. Visiting days with his mother had been forgettable, he ignored her for the most part when she was there. He dreaded it actually and spent a lot of time with

Demon on those days. He was a kid, but damn, his last memory of his mother reminded him of his first sight of Jolly. Scrawny, nervous, and unattractive, looking like she'd been crying. The two women didn't look alike at all. His mother was tall with blonde hair and his blue eyes.

If his father did that shit to her, it was no wonder she didn't try to fix her appearance before coming for a visit.

Another thing crossed his mind, Demon's mother lived with the old sonofabitch. She wasn't the type of woman to allow a man, any man, to hit her or call her names. What was going on with that? He didn't want to tell his friend about this, but if his father was treating Megan badly, and he knew there was a possibility he might be abusive to her, and didn't say anything. Well, he'd kill the fucker himself.

Gladys was waiting at the main entrance to the hospital when he drove up, so he didn't bother to park the car. He opened the door from inside and grinned at the little lady. "Hey, pretty lady, wanna go for a ride? I got candy." He wiggled his eyebrows and she choked on laughter as she climbed in. "I may have exaggerated about the candy, but I can still take you for a ride."

"How'd the campground fare while I was playing nursemaid to George the misogynist? I heard that several people were brought in by ambulance last night and the night before. And," She looked to see what his reaction was to the newest bit of gossip, "Luella, the nurse in the surgical wing where George was, told me Violet

203

Sanders was killed in a freak accident. It looks like her son, Abel, was driving their pick-up, and somehow didn't see his mother when he ran into her, pinning her between his truck and a tree. He claims that someone jumped him in the dark after church and took him and his mother out into the fire lanes off the highway. He told the sheriff he was drugged and passed out. His unknown assailant must have killed his mother and set him in the driver's seat to take the blame.

"Luella heard it from that deputy Kenneth Paul. He told her they found all kinds of drugs behind the seat, and the only drugs in his system were marijuana and traces of meth. They also found two handguns, with the serial numbers filed off, and an old sniper's rifle that appeared to have been recently fired. When they went to the house, there was stuff for a meth lab in the basement, and some stolen property.

"Luella said that Kenneth was the officer that found them this morning around dawn after he got a call about a suspicious noise coming from the woods. Some guy had a flat tire, and changed it during the storm. He said his wife and kids were in the car, so he was more concerned for them than something that sounded like a woman screaming during a storm." She should have known he wouldn't react, even though she'd told him everything with dramatic effect and the whole shebang. At least Georgie had frowned and became thoughtful when she shared the information with him.

"Now that's a damn shame, a pillar of the community struck down by her own kid." Knight wondered if that had something to do with the *things to see to*", crazy Charlie had been talking about last night. Come to think about it, Pressley had done a quick disappearing act soon after Charlie left the building too. He glanced at Gladys, knowing she was trying to get some sign from him the Bastards had been responsible for the demise of the county's number one busy body. "It seems Heaven is getting another righteous bible thumper to grace its gates."

Gladys might have bought his pseudo sympathetic comments if she hadn't seen his sly grin. "I guess you're right, after all, but since one of the handguns was in Violet's purse with her prints on it, a person would be forgiven if they speculated about the woman's religious standing."

Gladys wondered how bad a woman had to be, that virtually everyone that's ever heard of her could feel no sympathy at her untimely death. The funeral would be a big one, mostly because people would show up to make sure she was dead.

Knight helped Gladys out of the Mustang, and she didn't ask him why he was being such a gentleman. Most of the bikers had always treated her well, even curbing their language most of the time. If they ever heard her when something was frustrating her, or she hit her thumb instead of the nail she was attempting to hammer in the wall, they might think twice about the lady tag.

Demon was sitting in front of the TV in a towel, while Jolly was washing his clothes and baking cookies. The scene looked innocent enough, but from the whisker burns and purple bruising on Jolly's neck, it was obvious more than cookie baking and lounging had happened.

Gladys looked at Jolly's pink cheeks and raised her eyebrows, but didn't tease the younger woman. The attraction between Jolly and the two men was pretty much a done deal when they met. Even Future, with her screwy sense of "seeing" since pregnancy, had seen it. The hickeys on her neck were the biker's version of a dog pissing on a tree, claiming it. The thought made her grin.

Instead of teasing Jolly, she zeroed in on the giant redhead lounging on her sofa. "Are you trying to give me a heart attack?" He grinned at her and acted like he was going to pull the towel away from his lap until he saw Jolly narrowing her eyes and reconsidered.

"No, ma'am, I've been wearing the same damn clothes for two days, and the princess was nice enough to toss them into the wash. Since neither one of you have anything I could wear, it's the towel or nothing. I chose nothing, but she," he pointed at Jolly, who was hiding her head in the fridge, "made me wear this. She said if I wanted to sit on the furniture, I had to cover up."

Gladys passed Jolly on her way to her own room, and leaned down to whisper, "Spoilsport," before leaving the room.

Knight tossed Demon his duffle of clothes, and kept walking into the kitchen to hug Jolly. "Everything okay?" She nodded and returned the hug. "I need to borrow the car again for a few hours if you don't mind? I promise to take you for a ride on the chopper when we get it out of the woods. I've got a few Prospects coming over to cut up the rest of that tree later today. I need to take Demon with me, but we'll be back tonight, then we need to talk."

How he managed to make a demand sound like a request was truly an art form. Was it the tone of his voice? Or maybe it was the scorching kiss he'd left on her lips. Whichever it was, she told him to drive carefully, and bring her car back in one piece.

Demon pulled his jeans on right there in the living room since Gladys wasn't there at the time, and Jolly thought it was a damn shame to cover up all of that skin. It was probably for the best the men were leaving for a while. She needed to call her parents today. It felt strange even thinking the word parents, with an s.

Gladys finished her shower and looked in the unforgiving full length mirror on the wall. Very early this morning, Georgie woke up with a hard-on and saw she was in the room with him sleeping in a Naugahyde recliner. She woke when he cleared his throat, but she didn't notice the buttons on her top had come undone and she was showing him a good portion of her breasts encased in pink lace. She'd began buttoning up when he demanded that she stop doing that, "Don't hide those beauties from me, woman, come here and let me see them up close." Some bug must have crawled up her ass, because she went to him. She was tired of being alone, she was in need of a man's admiration, and since her and Ralph hadn't had sex since they'd first met and enjoyed a three year fling, she relied on the battery powered assistance to achieve an orgasm. It wasn't the same as strong arms and a warm body.

Georgie had finally let loose and pulled her down on the narrow bed. He ended up somehow with his torso hanging over hers, and his mouth filled with her nipple. His hand had slipped inside the waistband of her yoga pants and straight to her slit. Her hand found his erection, and she measured his length and breadth with her fingers and palm, working him slowly as his hips pushed his prick into her touch. It had taken only a couple of minutes before he brought her to pleasure, and shortly afterwards, her hand became drenched in his cum.

She felt her cheeks heat up as she remembered getting up from the bed and going into his bathroom to clean her hands and bring a warm damp cloth to clean him up. He laid back and tried to entice her into exploring him with her mouth, but she wasn't about to be caught like that in a public place. What they'd already done would have mortified her if they'd been caught.

The ass actually thought she was giving in and accepting his self-imposed role as her boss afterwards. When she told him, "I'm not denying that I'm attracted to you, there's no reason to hide it, but I want a man who respects me, not one who needs to be my boss." That didn't go over well—not by a long shot—and they ended up in another yelling match until she grew tired of the arguing. She didn't bother to say goodbye, she picked up her bag of clothes and her purse and walked out the door.

Over hot coffee and freshly baked cookies, the women caught up on the past few days. Gladys told her that Georgie was still an ass with his shitty attitude about women. "Not that I want to speculate about his momma, but I bet that woman stayed home and never said shit if she had a mouthful."

She waited a few minutes as they enjoyed the mid-morning snack. "So tell me, are they as good as their reputations say they are?"

Jolly knew what she was talking about and figured it must have been obvious they'd done more than just stayed in the same house together. She grinned at the memories of what they'd done. "Those two are *A*-fucking-mazing. I was walking bowlegged!" Laughing at the way Gladys fanned herself, she told her about Demon splitting the two big piles of wood out back. "You'll have enough firewood to keep the house heated for the whole winter. His hands were a bloody mess from the broken blisters, but I found some antibiotic cream and wrapped them, so he will be fine in a few days. Men are such dipshits sometimes, but at least he was a productive dipshit, right?"

The news of the split wood was welcome. She had wondered how she would get it all split into pieces small enough for her to carry in the little wheelbarrow from the woodpile to the back porch where there was a lean-to just for keeping the wood dry for her winter fires. The wood stove helped keep the gas bills down and made it a little more affordable to live out here in the cold months.

"Well, why don't we take a tour of the campsites and cabins to make sure they got through the storms alright? Just remember to leave the two occupied cabins alone unless they ask for something. I told you about the people before and they're very self-sufficient, but from time to time they run into a problem." Jolly met her at the door after putting on her shoes and grabbing her phone.

CHAPTER TWENTY ONE

Demon hadn't asked where they were headed until they drove through Donnell, a small town west of Prindale. "You mind telling me where we're going? Or do you have a surprise party planned for me? Seeing how my birthday's a few months away, it would be a total surprise." He frowned when Knight pulled over to the side of the road by the river and told him they needed to talk.

The big men got out of the car and Knight sat his ass down on the riverbank without saying anything until Demon joined him. That's when he began to talk. He told him about the conversation with Charlie and why he'd called his mother.

"He kept looking at me like I should know what he was talking about when he said stuff about strong women. I didn't even know what the fuck the old fart was saying until around four this morning. I thought about it, and ended up calling my mother. I had to call her sister to get the number, and she wasn't happy about being woken up so early, but she gave me the number and said she was hoping I was calling to tell them that my dad was dead." He shook his head and tossed a rock into the swiftly flowing water.

"You and your mom moved into the trailer park after my mom left, so you probably don't remember her much unless you saw her the few times she visited me."

He told Demon about the call he'd made to his mother, and the news he was still trying to come to grips with. "I knew he was a mean fucker, but the idea of how mean he was to her, that's damn hard to swallow. I want to go over there and beat his head in, but he was a good father to me. The women he brought home never stayed long, you know that. I was too busy being a kid to pay attention at the time, but when I took the time to sift through the memories, I can remember my mother's face when I got called into the house at night for supper. On those nights there was always a big home cooked meal waiting for me. She always looked like she'd been crying, and she moved like a puppet on strings. I ignored her, mostly 'cause the old man constantly told me she didn't want us and left to be with her boyfriends. He would say to me right in front of her that he had to force her to come and see me, so if I had anything I wanted to say to her, I should say it then because who knew when she'd come back. I remember one time she raised a pan toward his head when he said that, but she saw me watching her and put it down.

"I swear, man, she kept thanking me for calling her, and I feel like shit on a shoe for ignoring her all of these years. I could hear her crying and shit, and fuckin' saying how she never forgot me, and prayed to talk to me again. Thanking me for crissakes." He hurled a fist sized rock at the water and watched the splash, but it did nothing to soothe his emotions.

"Now I'm worried about Megan, I can't imagine a woman as strong as your mom letting Wild Bill beat on her or treat her like shit, but the thought won't go away until I see her and know for certain she's okay. I thought about just making the old fucker disappear, but something inside me says not to." He turned to Demon, who had sat in silence through Knight spilling his guts. "I swear, if he's laid a hand on her, I'll kill him where I find him. You have my word on it."

Demon nodded his head, he already knew most of what his friend just told him. Well, he knew about Bill beating on Carla. Everyone in the trailer park knew but Knight. He didn't know about the rest, but he'd already had one talk with his mother about the man's temper, and she swore he must've changed. After hearing the rest of the story, he grew concerned himself. His mother was one of the strongest people he knew, but who knew what she'd put up with if she felt she had to. He stood, dusted the dirt off his ass, and headed for the car.

Before Knight put the Mustang in gear, he told him, "If Bill has touched my mother in any hurtful way, or is verbally abusive to her, he's dead. He will disappear, and she'll be moving to Prindale. As far as I know, he and your mother are still legally married, but if he has life insurance, she gets it. It won't make up for all the years of hell she went through, but it might help her retirement. I already have mom listed as an employee in my LLC, so she has a retirement package."

This was news to Knight, and he grilled his friend for the rest of the drive about making such arrangements for Carla. They'd been best friends and shared just about everything, but their investments and money was their own business.

*****

The small house was situated away from the sidewalk about fifty foot, and they could hear someone in the garage listening to a country and western station on the radio. The same station must have been playing in the house, because they could hear it through the open windows. Demon went to the door and Knight kept going to the garage.

He made sure he made enough noise so as not to startle his volatile father. The man had fast reflexes for an old guy, and he didn't want to get shot for visiting. Bill was rebuilding a motor and when he saw Knight, his smile was genuine. "Hey, boy, it's about time you come for a visit."

He pumped some hand cleaner into the palm of one hand and rubbed the stuff in, making a nasty looking mess of his hands until he grabbed a few paper towels from the roll, and wiped them clean. Then he went to the back of the garage and brought back a couple of sodas for them.

"So what brings you all the way out here in the middle of the week? Not that I don't like seein' you, but you usually call before you show up."

Knight took a swallow of his cola and looked directly at his father. "I called my mother this morning."

Bill looked down and nodded his head, then looked back to his son. "Yeah, I should've said something, but I figured to leave the past dead and buried. I should've known it'd come back and bite me on the ass." He shook his head and closed his eyes before pulling the bandanna off his head. There were two nasty looking lines on the side of his head that appeared to be surgical scars.

"It's a short story with a long history. I owe that woman more than an apology, but I was sure she didn't want me to find her, so you can tell her what I'm going to tell you. You had left boot camp for overseas before I found out I had a fucking growth on my brain. A week after you left, I went in and had surgery. They thought it was brain cancer, but it turned out to be an abnormal growth. They said it'd been there for years growing, and that I wouldn't have noticed unless I had the same tests they used to find it. When I started getting headaches and 'rages' as they called them, I should've gone into the doctor and told him."

He swallowed a mouthful of the liquid and his mouth worked a little before he continued, "The 'rages', that's a technical term, did you know that? Anyway, I've had them since I was a kid, probably eighteen or nineteen years old. That's when the doc said the tumor probably started to grow. I was like a fuckin' grizzly bear with a sore paw. Mean as a man could be. Each year it got worse, and I got used to it, got used to being an evil sonofabitch. I met your mom when we traveled through the south. I picked her up for a date and just never found the time to take her back. You know we got shackled because you were on the way. Carla was always attractive, beautiful really. I hated it when I had to bust a couple of the brothers for trying to get her to look their way. I started taking it out on her when the Prez took me aside and warned me they were getting' tired of my shit.

"The last time I saw your mother, let's just say I'm glad she didn't come back. Not because of you or her, but because I probably would have killed the woman, and she'd never done a thing except love me and you. I used you as a way to blackmail her, and I understand if you want to beat my ass now for the way I acted, but I can't change what happened, and neither can you.

"Long history short, you and Demon weren't around to help me learn to do a lot of things again. You boys would have laughed to see my big ass stumbling around when I had to relearn to walk. I was in rehab for almost a year, and physical therapy for even longer at home. Demon wrote and asked me to look in on Megan if I got a chance and I called her once I could speak without drooling all over my damned chin. Hell, boy, I was still pissin' my pants and not knowing I needed to go before I felt the fuckin' piss soaking my legs. We talked a few times a week, and she came to see me when I had to have the second operation because they hadn't gotten all the growth the first time, she moved in after I got to come home.

"Megan is a hell of a woman, and she don't put up with any orneriness from me." His grin made it plain that he loved her for her feisty ways, and Knight lost the budding fear for the woman that treated him as if he was one of her own. "If you get lucky and find the right woman, you better make sure you don't fuck up your life like I did mine and hurt her so bad she leaves you. I had to almost die twice before I found another woman worth calling mine who would tolerate my ass for more than five minutes."

Before he left, Bill took him aside and asked him to tell his mother that he was sorry for all of the hurt he'd caused. "You tell her that I can't undo what I did to her, hell, I will pay for it for the rest of my life, because the truth is, I remember most of what happened. I ain't the same man anymore, and I hope her life is good."

Knight nodded and promised to return in a few weeks. Demon drove them to the hospital to see how Big D was doing, and while Knight was busy talking with Future, Demon took another elevator to see how the woman, Barbara, was doing. When he stepped off the elevator, he saw Fuller sitting with the kid and his granny talking. He hit the elevator button again and stepped back inside. *Good enough for now*. Maybe the family could finally get together, even if Fuller was doing it for economic reasons. He'd be sure to keep an eye on the situation, just in case.

Future told them Big Dog would be going home by the end of the week, and she would give him a ride. They promised to help if she needed it, but Demon decided to tackle the issue of the club's hunting process. "Look, let me clarify something for you 'cause you're as stubborn as Big D. What we do is no more or less than what any private detective agency does. Someone wants someone found, and we find them. We get paid for finding them, and we check out why we're looking for them. If a person is hiding from a dangerous situation, we don't take the gig. We have our codes, Future, so don't think we're tossing innocents to the wolves. Price isn't always the factor." He nodded at her and left the room to meet up with Knight in the parking lot.

Demon filled Knight in on Jolly's story on the way back to the campground. They both decided they liked William's way of dealing with bastards like Porter and James. To Knight, the story explained a lot about Jolly's looks and behavior when they'd first met. It also explained why she'd come back as an outgoing though slightly nervous young woman.

Knight gave a short laugh, "You do realize that my father's name is William?"

Demon nodded, "Yeah, but somehow I can't see William Kelly and Wild Bill measuring cocks over who gets to be called what. I love your dad like the father I never had, but if William Kelly got pissed at him, dear old dad is fucked."

Four bikes and a pick-up towing a log splitter were parked in the lot by the main house of the campground when they pulled the Mustang to a stop. Donnie and Poppa were sitting on the porch with plates of deep fried chicken and potato salad. "You boys better hurry in there and get a plate. Mick, Show, and Larry just drove up a few minutes ago."

Jolly was laughing at something Show was telling her, and Gladys was sitting next to them at the kitchen breakfast bar talking. Knight immediately began to feel territorial and pulled her head back to give her a warning kiss. He had to prove to them that she was his property. Show laughed and stood. "No intent, brother." He shook his head still laughing, grabbed his plate of food, and left to find a spot on the porch with friendlier company.

Gladys took her plate and left the breakfast bar allowing the men to sit on either side of Jolly. Seeing the way they were staring at her new friend gave her a serious case of the envies. It was the way Jolly looked back at them that counted to her. The entire room could see the girl was more than smitten, she was ready to snap the lock on her heart and brain, just as the men were fastening their own shackles around her.

That's how it should be, a man had to give his woman a reason to lock down other than sex or security. He needed to value her, just like she valued him. Gladys kept her face turned from the people in the room and set her plate in the fridge. She practically ran to her room, shut the door quietly, and threw herself on her bed, before she let her tears fall.

CHAPTER TWENTY TWO

Jolly was thankful they'd used paper plates to feed everyone. She drained the deep fryer and spent an hour cleaning the kitchen and tables in the house. Knight and Demon left with the rest of the men to get their bikes, and help them with transporting and unloading the wood from the big tree.

She'd been thoroughly kissed and felt-up by both men, but her pretend complaints drew smiles instead of scowls. She knew it wouldn't be long before she heard from them again. She fixed a half pot of Gladys's favorite coffee, and warmed the woman's plate before going to her room and tapping on the door.

"Everyone's gone now, Gladys, I heated your dinner and made coffee if you feel like coming out and talking." She left the plate in the microwave, and poured herself a cup, mixing a teaspoon of sugar and a dollop of milk into the mug. She was sitting on the quiet porch when Gladys came out with the food and her own mug.

"Thanks for not microwaving the potato salad, I would have barfed if the stuff was ruined. I owe you an apology for slipping away like that. I felt too emotional to deal with men's bullshit and needed a break, but I'm fine now."

After she ate all she could, she sat back and told Jolly what she was planning to do. "I think I'll start looking for either a partner, or just outright sell the campground. It's too much for me to deal with by myself, and I still need an income during the winter

220

off-season. This place is just too big for me to rattle around in alone. I have a bit in savings, but I can't travel at all in the summertime, and I'm not much for sitting around watching my fingers twiddle, so I need a seasonal job." She shook her head before refocusing on Jolly.

"Have you decided what you plan to do about the men? Will you take them on, or are you thinking about bowing out and going back to college or something?"

"I'd like to give you an answer, but so far, I have no idea what they want exactly. I made up my mind that I wasn't going to waste my time playing coy. I'm head over heels for them, even Knight, and he's an asshole at times. I still can't figure out why so many people are afraid of Demon. He's just your average overgrown variety of Yeti. Believe it or not, both men say I can stand to gain a few pounds. Whatever I decide to do, I promise that you will know as soon as I do. I won't leave you hanging."

They talked about the campground and the cabins. "The first guests will be here on Friday night. Also we need to put fresh linens in the cabins, and make sure the place is sprayed for spiders, just in case. One year Ralph forgot to spray and we were hearing screams all week until they left and he had a chance to spray before the next campers came in. City people rarely see spiders like we have out here in the country. One woman swore that an innocent wood spider was a scorpion, and she wanted her money back. I started leaving those charts with the "Know That Bug" theme taped to the cupboard doors. Since then I added a Know That Fish, and Know that Wild Animal."

They finally went to bed around ten thirty that night, planning to get the cabins in order for occupation tomorrow.

*****

During Church, Demon made the big announcement to a yawning crowd. "Knight and I decided to make Jolly Kelly our old lady, anybody have an objection? Her Bastards tag will be Princess." Aside from a few lewd remarks, there was nothing to discuss about their choice. She wouldn't have full membership privileges until she'd proven herself worthy, but she wouldn't be harassed by any of the single guys either.

The discussion about the recent demise of Violet and her son's arrest for murdering her was a hot topic, but no one claimed to know anything about the incident. The absences of Crazy Charlie and Pressley were explained away by Knight, who told them all that the two men were doing club business. Knight shook his head at the comment Heckle made about the peashooter that was found in the truck with Violet's boy.

"Are you serious? They found a fuckin' 338 LaPua. That bitch has a range of eighteen hundred yards, and when they match the bullets with that gun, his ass is going down for attempted murder on Big D, Georgie, Show, Demon, and me. I would give both of Chester's nuts for a gun like that, just to say I had one." Chester was a skinny brother with a spotty beard, and long greying hair. He was fried most days, and didn't give a shit about anything until you riled him up, or stole his stash of weed. He sat in the back and shot Knight the finger when he'd mentioned his nuts. They'd been gone since Nam.

The next morning, everyone around the club noted Georgie's return with a warm greeting and a lot of teasing about falling off his bike. Knight had already been to the campground and found out that Jolly was going to be busy all day, but they had a date for tonight. When he told Georgie that Gladys was thinking about selling the campground and moving out of the area, the man turned red, but stayed in his seat. He didn't tell the older brother that Jolly was thinking about buying half interest in the place if she could get the financing. She didn't want to go to the bank of daddy, and Knight respected her for that.

*****

Knight came to pick her up on the chopper, and she was happy they didn't go very far because her ass was not comfortable on the small patch of leather Knight called the Bitch Pad. She loved the feeling of freedom as the wind blew through her short hair and the late afternoon sunshine rejuvenated her tired body from her day's work.

They turned down a tree lined path not far from the campground that opened into a large yard. There was a small cabin on the property, they rode to it and Knight parked the bike. Demon's hog was already parked near the front door, and Knight grinned when she raised her eyebrows. "We wanted privacy to talk. Gladys is around at the camp, and there's no such thing as privacy at the club. This is the one place we can almost guarantee we won't be disturbed."

Inside the doorway, Demon waited for them, and she felt her heart crack a little more. She saw all the effort they'd gone to, to give her the hearts and flowers stuff. There was a heart shaped chocolate cake on the table, and a quart canning jar filled with black eyed Susan's and other wildflowers. A plain white candle was jammed into a beer bottle dripping wax onto a paper plate. There was an envelope on the table, and a present gift wrapped with the Sunday comics. Demon was watching for her reaction and she grinned at him.

"My goodness, did you guys bake a cake?" They shook their heads in tandem and she almost giggled. "It doesn't matter, this is perfect." She bent to the flowers and inhaled the scent of earth and seeing the purple clover, she knew where the sweet scent came from. "These are beautiful, thank you."

"We figured we would start this thing as if we mean to go on. If you want romance, we can do that, if you want hearts and flowers, we can do that too. If you want two men that are crazy about you, well that part's the easiest." Demon finished his declaration and took her left hand.

"I know I'm a jealous asshole sometimes. One day I'll tell you the story of a young boy who had a new woman living at his house every few months while he was a teenager. I want you to know, I'll do my damnedest to curb my territorial instincts, and you should know I will never hurt you. Demon too. You might get a spanking now and again, but I'll never take my fist to you or cause you to doubt my feelings for you in anyway."

He took her other hand and she nodded her head instead of trying to say something that'd come out like a rough choking sound. She cleared her throat, and "So, uh, you guys better be sure this is what you want, because when we enter into this commitment, I'll hold your feet to the fire myself if you so much as speculate about another woman. I know you're men and will look, but don't cheat. If you want out, tell me, I'll help you pack, no matter how much it might hurt at the time. I want a relationship with trust. I want the house, and kids. I want a dog." She was pulled into Knight's arms and kissed breathless while Demon stripped her shoes and jeans from her body. His big hands rolled her panties down at the same time as her jeans fell off her toes to the floor. Knight's hands unsnapped her bra, and began pulling the tank top over her head, the bra went with the t-shirt.

They had her naked in mere seconds, and they shucked their clothing just as quickly. She went to her knees and looked at the beautiful pricks in front of her face. She swallowed and licked her lips before latching onto Demon's wide prick. She didn't suck him inside of her mouth, instead she licked him, twirling her tongue around the silky flesh covering solid core muscle.

"Hey, wait a minute, we need to make this official." Knight handed her the gift and pulled her to her feet. "I'm not the most thoughtful man in the world, but for some reason I want to see this on you before we get down and dirty."

She opened the box and took out a beautifully worked leather vest. The name Princess was embroidered between Demon and Knight under the Bastards' skeleton logo. Demon took it and held it up for her to slip her arms in. "That's fuckin' hot," was his pronouncement.

Knight wanted the official words, and he asked her flat out, "Will you be our old lady and wear our cut?"

She looked around the small cabin, at the table with the bending candle and the cake, then at the two men that were sober faced, waiting for her answer.

"Do you promise to keep your dicks in your pants when I'm not around?" They nodded. "Will you promise to love me when I'm not so lovable, listen to what I want to say privately, and not humiliate me in front of your brothers just because the guys expect it?" Again the nodding heads. "Okay, it's like this, and this is my line in the sand. If you want out, tell me. If you're mad at someone else, don't expect me to be your whipping girl. If you're mad at me, tell me and we'll talk about it, I'm not a fortuneteller, and I can't read your minds." More nods and grins aimed her way. She took the vest off and hung it on the back of a chair, held out her hands and, "Let's find a comfortable spot and get you two naked."

EPILOGUE

Selma had called him twenty times in the past month, ever since she'd won the Judge's seat for the county, but Charlie hadn't listened to the voicemails. He'd cut her loose to follow her dreams, and wanted her to be happy in her new position and life. Now this pissant sheriff's deputy was asking if he'd seen her anytime in the last three days. What the fuck? Someone had been threatening his Selma and he'd ignored her calls asking for his help. He was a lowdown sonofabitch. After talking to the cop, Charlie went to his room and listened to the voicemails. His blood heated hearing the sultry tone of her voice, and gradually cooled turning to ice when he heard the last two desperate messages. Thankfully Selma was smart enough to give him a name. He rubbed his face with both hands, and began forming his plan.

ABOUT THE AUTHOR

RYDER DANE

I write about MC Groups aka Biker Books, because I've lived with Motorcycles my entire life. It made me smile when a reviewing reader said that there was a realistic feel to my writing! Having been an "Old Lady" since I was 19 gives me the advantage of using a few real details of MC life. I am very happy to bring readers my stories and having them invest in my characters' lives.

Website: <u>Ryderdane.com</u>

<u>Books by Ryder Dane</u>
Big Dog (Burning Bastards MC Book 1)
Nomad's Fall (Burning Bastards MC Book 2)
Charlie's Heart
(Burning Bastards MC Series Book 3)

Sanctuary Within the Breed
(Lucifer's Breed MC Book 1)
Integrity Has No Bounds
(Lucifer's Breed MC Book 2)
Starting Over (Lucifer's Breed MC Book 3)